Death on Coffin Island

MICHELE NUTWELL

Michele Nutwell
2007

DEATH ON
COFFIN ISLAND

A Folly Beach Mystery

2007

Death on Coffin Island

ACKNOWLEDGMENTS

This book would not have materialized without the persistence of my husband, who said keep writing, keep writing, keep writing. Thank-you, Steve.

To the people who read the first drafts and encouraged me so very much, thanks to my mom, Ruth Tarr, my sister, Suzanne Wallace, my adoptive parents David and Barbara May, Jacky McGowan for the editing and Fran Varady British series insight; you have all been a blessing.

Thanks to my dad, Mike Tarr, for the cool last name Palevac (paluhvac). I finally got to use it.

To the fine folks who inhabit the island of Folly, thanks for the inspiration. It's been a wild ride.

To the professionals at Booksurge, you have been a pleasure to work with.

Finally, to my children, Logan, Stephen and Brianna. I hope this serves as encouragement to you all that dreams do come true.

PROLOGUE

The world as I knew it changed that day. There was no warning, no blast of trumpets from on high, no sense of being in the wrong place at the wrong time. Nothing. I think of the time before that day as normal life, and after it, as abnormal life. In hindsight, I was quite enjoying life in that normal time, until I learned what abnormal was all about. And now I'm pissed.

Don't get me wrong. It's much better being among the living. It's just that my peaceful, mundane and somewhat predictable life has forever been altered. Not only that, I now find myself with the unpleasantness of reporters in my face. Reporters can be a real bitch to deal with. Being one myself, I have firsthand knowledge.

My name is Kell Palevac, and I work for *The Archipelago*, a small newspaper covering Charleston, South Carolina, better known as the Holy City. I'm the reporter for the city of Folly Beach, better known as The Edge of America, although it was referred to as Coffin Island back in the good ol' days of cholera. I landed my job at *The Archipelago* fresh out of the College of Charleston five years ago, making it a whopping nine years I have claimed this town as home. It's longer than I've lived anywhere in my life.

My father was a consultant on Latin-American matters, and so the family traversed North and South America at a whirlwind pace, the four of us stopping just long enough to catch our breath before heading off to yet another locale. My mother, a historical writer, was amazingly adept at doing her research, writing, raising us and moving without missing a beat. My brother Aidan and I were born during her Celtic phase, hence the charming Celtic names. Mine comes from The Book of Kells. I've always been grateful we didn't come along during her later Native American Indian phase. Admirable warriors that they were, I can't quite swallow the idea of going through life as Yellow Corn Ear Maiden and claiming a brother named He Who Skins Squirrels.

While attending journalism school in Charleston I took the opportunity to explore the famous city and the islands surrounding it. Marshlands and pluff mudd form a backdrop for the area's many bridges. Charleston connects to James Island by way of two bridges and Folly Beach connects to James Island by only one. Once you get there, the locals say, why would you ever want to leave? After residing on Folly for the past five of my nine years in Dixieland, I tend to agree. All told, I love my job covering this eclectic little island and was humming along quite nicely. But that was then and this, as they say, is now.

Reporters hounding me is a new one. The only other time I was asked for my opinion from the press was when I was ten and living in Sao Paulo, Brasil. The subject then was the practice of women selling their natural blonde hair to a Brasilian artist obsessed with golden locks and who wove them into gigantic murals. At the market with my blonde mother and equally blonde brother, I was stopped by a man with a microphone, another with a television camera. The reporter stroked my long, unruly, natural blonde mane and asked if I would sell my hair to the apparently illustrious artist in the news. "Que linda," he purred, holding the wavy length up for the camera's eye. Soon I was surrounded by dark-haired, dark-eyed Brasilians clamoring for a look at me, or my hair. Scared shitless they were going to descend upon me with scissors, I kneed the reporter in the balls with all my ten-year-old might. I wish I could do the same to the flock of idiots hovering over me today each time I step outside. Instead, I'll do what I do best. I'll write the damn story myself. Then I'll give it to each and every one of the obnoxious morons hungry for a comment. Then I'll knee them in the balls.

CHAPTER ONE

I suppose if you wanted to see what my life was like when it was normal it would be best to just start on the day it switched to abnormal. The alarm buzzed entirely too loudly for my liking. There was no sunlight streaming in my windows to wake me up as was usual. I swatted at the source of the offending noise, squinted at the numbers displayed and was immediately relieved. A mistake. There was no way I was getting up at five a.m. Apparently I'd set the clock wrong the night before. I eased back under the beckoning covers, groggy and grumpy at being so rudely awakened.

"Shit. Shit, shit, shit," I muttered when I remembered, indeed it was I who had set the alarm for this ungodly hour, and on purpose, too. I reached for my glasses and knocked over a cup of water. Fur flew as something squeaked in distress.

"Sorry, Sampson." My long-haired black cat glared at me. He would have looked pretty funny all wet like that if it hadn't been so early. He shook and stalked off. Great, now my cat has an attitude, I thought. He'll be shredding my papers by midday.

"Okay, Kell, you wanted to get in an early run? Start functioning," I ordered myself. Sometimes it actually works, talking myself into these daybreak ordeals. After the pizza I inhaled the night before, it was actually quite easy jump starting my brain. Exercise is what I do to prevent having to give up pizza. And ice cream. And red wine. It's a long list.

Miraculously, the coffee was brewing. I love it when I remember to preset it the night before. Grabbing a cup with real sugar I then doused it with nonfat cream, contemplating how the two balanced each other out. By the time I had finished it my contacts were in, my shoes were tied and I'd snapped my ever-present cell phone to my blue running shorts. I don't think all the synapses in my head were firing yet, but usually by the time I finished my four-mile jog they were pretty well in order.

It was still dark outside but I knew the sun would rise as I set out. On the mornings I actually get up this early it's always a treat. There's a whole lot of truth to the beauty of southern skies.

"Fred," I whispered as I crouched down. "Wake up, Fred. It's morning. Come on, let's go for a run."

No response. Fred is not a morning person. Fred is really not much of a daytime person either, and appears to be quite content to sleep the day away. I ruffled his hair. "Come on, Fred, get up. You're coming with me." I pushed and grunted, and he unwillingly got to his feet. Yawning, he looked like he would gladly eat me for breakfast.

"Gross, you really do have dog breath, and you need a bath. I promise I'll take you to the groomers real soon, okay? Let's go, boy."

With that I snapped the leash on my 150-pound Great Dane. I rescued him from a salvage yard I did an article on two years ago. The owner of the salvage yard, Bubba Pinckney, had purchased Fred to use as a guard dog for the property. Fred, however, had other plans. He had no use for chasing away would-be thieves, and at the time I met him, he was being shipped off to the dog pound by the highly agitated Mr. Pinckney.

Now, remember this is still the time of relative normalcy, a point I make to remind myself of the so utterly beautiful simplicity of my life at that stage in the game. I notice now what a really easy time I had of it. The pressing item on the agenda for that morning was my meeting with Bonnie McLeod, President of Adopt a Pet and wife of the mayor of our little town. She loves me. This is mostly because I share her love of animals and am usually at her disposal when it comes to whatever she feels is newsworthy in regards to all things furry. It doesn't hurt that I wrote a rather complimentary feature story on her husband, either. Bonnie's pretty cool in a rather neurotic way, but she has this thing for early-morning appointments, which is a strike against her in my book, but hey, who's counting?

Fred yawned again, and I moved quickly before he could lie back down. We greeted the pre-dawn morning and walked across the street to the beach. I remember the fog, which was fairly typical before the sun rose, and the sense of stillness. It's funny, because I don't remember any seagulls squawking or even the sound of the waves although they were both surely there. Maybe it's my sense of the macabre over the way the morning turned out, but it was sort of spooky. That I definitely remember.

Since the wind was coming out of the west, I started out in that direction. I always plan my runs that way, so after I turn around I have the wind at my back. Makes it easier with a push from Mother Nature to finish up. Two mile this way puts me just on the other side of the pier by the Holiday Inn, Folly's only hotel. It's an easy route, two miles up and two miles back. Fred and I were off in a flash.

"Come on, fur face. We're running here, not going for a morning stroll," I yelled as Fred fell behind. What the hell, pulling 150 pounds of practically dead weight had to help burn more calories. The hard-packed sand felt good under my feet.

After about ten minutes I had had enough of the extra caloric advantages my companion was giving me. I had begun to keep Fred leased when we ran. It still horrifies me to think about the time we were lazily walking along the water's edge, me looking for shells and Fred, well, just being Fred. He was harmlessly sniffing the sand, unleashed. I'd only had him about a month and quickly discovered he didn't leave my side, so I thought he was fine just meandering along with me. Next thing I hear are shrieks of gibberish as a brightly dressed family of five are flattened out in the sand, hands covering their heads. Fred was actually running circles around them and barking his head off. Till this day I have no idea why he did that. All I can come up with is that he must have known they were tourists.

Tired of dragging Fred behind me, I let go of his leash. "You better keep up, buddy."

There weren't any other joggers or walkers on the beach. My legs stretched out as the pier got closer, and I could feel the sun on my back as it rose. Breathing hard, I dashed under the 25-foot-wide structure, then slowed a bit and did a backwards jog so I could locate Fred.

"Fur face, you are definitely getting faster," I hollered. Amazingly, he was only a few feet behind. I turned to face forward again and got to the rock I knew marked two miles.

"Good job, Kell, now turn around and do two more." The encouraging words to myself had diminished effect because all I could really hear was a strange howling sound coming out of my dog. Fred was under the pier next to a piling, down near the edge of the water. He was making a sound I'd never heard come out of him before, sort of a wailing noise. He was so big I couldn't see what he had found.

I jogged back towards him. "What is it, boy? You scared of a blue crab or something? Does one have you by the paw?"

Fred didn't answer, but he did continue the rather pitiful sounding howl. I ran up to him so fast I bumped into him.

Sweaty and panting, I looked around his large bulk. I wished I hadn't.

"What in the name of-------" I screamed. I stared and screamed a little more.

A surfboard was attached to the piling, floating peacefully in the Atlantic's break. Attached to the surfboard was a body, stretched out and floating peacefully, too. It was a female. Her blue eyes stared vacantly up towards the pier's underside. Her hair was long and blondish, fanning out around the board like a halo. She wore a purple rashguard and nothing else.

I don't know how long I stood there. Time froze. Fred howled and wailed. I snapped out of it and promptly did what any good reporter would do. I puked my guts out. Then I unhitched my cell phone from my side and called my editor.

CHAPTER TWO

T he City of Folly's finest men in blue arrived quickly, which is not a miracle as the whole island is only six miles long and about a mile wide. Where else could they be, for heaven's sake?

Officer's Dan Jacoby and Mark McClellan were headed towards us at a rather frenetic pace. Well, for them. In all my years here I had never seen an officer move so fast. Remember, this town of mine is pretty laid back. Nobody turns up dead.

"Palevac, what in the hell is going on here," McClellan panted.

He didn't look so good. Truthfully, he never looks good, with greasy hair and a bulbous nose rivaled only by the bulging belly currently heaving and straining against his tight uniform. A button popped off his shirt and smacked me in the cheek. To add insult to injury, he wiped at the sweat on his brow and flung it carelessly in my direction. Reigning in the wicked thoughts racing through my head, I granted mercy. Please, dear Lord, I silently prayed, do not let him die now. Another time, perhaps, I couldn't resist thinking, but not now. I couldn't handle two dead bodies at once.

Officer McClellan continued his assault. "Why did you call your paper and not us?"

I noticed his face was the same reddish shade as his greasy hair and equally oily. Fred and I were curled up into one another some distance from the surfboard with the blonde attached. I wished she were just sleeping.

Jacoby was on his knees, maybe hoping the same thing as he checked for a pulse. His radio crackled and he called in to the station and then walked to where Fred, McClellan and I were planted.

"Seriously, Palevac, you should have called us immediately, not your editor. Lucky for you she had the presence of mind to call the authorities." McClellan's eyes bulged and he looked like all 200 pounds of him were going to explode.

"Sorry, I have her on speed dial," I snapped, sounding a whole lot feistier than I felt. "She's dead, right," I directed at Jacoby.

"Affirmative. Ms. DeWinter called at 5:51 a.m. to report your phone call to her. Had you just discovered the body, Kell?" Jacoby asked gently. Boyishly handsome with his sandy hair styled in a little boy regular, he is our chief of police's nephew and brand new to the force. It was no secret he had a crush on me, which was flattering. And I had worked hard to get him to stop calling me ma'am. I understand he's barely twenty-one and feels at the ripe old age of twenty-seven I am deserving of his Southern male chivalry, but I was no Scarlett O'Hara and it simply made me feel old.

"Yeah, I guess it was a reflex action, calling her with any breaking news," I said. It did sound pretty shabby, I thought, staring at the now officially declared dead woman. I shivered and snuggled up closer to Fred. He was in an obvious state of shock. Every once in a while he let out a tentative howl and then sighed heavily. I had to get my act together for my dog.

I stood up, brushed the sand off my rear end and tried to look like I was with it. I trotted after the officers towards the victim.

Jacoby was kneeling again, peering closely at the face. "Her facial features aren't indistinguishable yet, so she hasn't been in the water long. We'll have to wait for the coroner, of course, but I'd say she died of strangulation."

McClellan and I leaned over in unison, angling for a view. There was a deep, ugly red welt around the woman's neck. She couldn't have been more than twenty years old, I thought. Pretty, with the deep tan of someone who sees a lot of the sun.

"Could we, um, cover her with a towel or something," I asked. She looked so cold and exposed lying there.

"Sure, sure, of course we will," Jacoby said. "I'll get something from the squad car. Everyone else will be arriving shortly." He pinched the bridge of his nose between his fingers. I knew this must be his first dead body, too.

Sirens squealed as he departed for the promised covering. Here comes the backup crew, although I didn't know what they were going to do. The poor girl was confirmed dead, why in the world did they have to come screaming in with sirens now?

"McClellan, any positive ID yet? What was the time of death? Method, motive, and why in the hell didn't that reporter call us first." Chief Strom Stoney stormed the scene. Must be his first body, too, I thought. I tried to stay invisible. Fred made it a little difficult.

"Palevac." McClellan whirled on me so fast I jumped, narrowly escaping the bits of sweat flying in my direction. "What is going on here? How come you found this body? How come nobody else saw it first?"

Well, I thought to myself, news has been a little slow lately so I thought I'd spice things up a bit, you arrogant asshole. Glaring at McClellan, I turned to face the chief. I noticed we were about the same height.

"Chief Stoney, this has been a big shock to me. I was jogging and my dog found her. I don't know why I didn't see her when I ran by, but then I did and I called my editor, and I guessed she called you guys. I'm so glad you're here." Gushing did not sit well with me. The chief looked like an angry, miniature version of McClellan, minus the red hair and nose thing. His ears were rather red, however, and in my present state of controlled hysteria I could swear there was steam hissing out of them.

"You!" he barked, pointing in my direction. "Go to the station and give a statement. Do not, I repeat, DO NOT, write about this yet. We have to advise next of kin." He ran his hand through what was left of his graying hair. For the second time in one day someone looked at me like they could eat me for breakfast.

"Sir, do we have any idea who she is," I tried.

For a short man he could throw out some pretty devastating looks. I withered. Normally, I do not wither. Apparently a dead body had thrown a wrench into my façade.

"Go to the station. Do not pass go. Do not talk to your cronies. Do not call me today. Got it?"

I stared at the imaginary puffs of smoke steaming out of Chief Stoney's ears, blinking my eyes to dispense with the image and calmly met the gaze of his flashing blue eyes.

"Well sir, yes, I'll go to the station, of course I will. After that I have to go to work and see what Alex, uh, Ms. DeWinter wants me to do," I said.

"Why in the hell did a fucking reporter have to find the first dead person here in thirty fucking years," he muttered to no one. He turned away to deal with the others who had arrived and were examining the body. I was dismissed.

CHAPTER THREE

Fred and I walked slowly back home, neither of us in a very talkative mood. The sun was high in the east by now, casting shimmering rays of light through the early morning clouds that would burn off by mid-day. The low tide revealed several sand dollars, treasures that normally beckon to me. I didn't bother them.

"Fur face, you did good," I said to Fred. Eyes downcast, he kept bumping into me as we walked. At moments like this I knew he wished he were a poodle or some other tiny bundle that could be carried. The ring of my cell phone startled us both.

"Kell here."

"Where are you and why haven't you called me back yet," asked my highly organized and efficient editor. "We have a scoop on this thing. Get to the office right away."

"I'm just about home, Alex. I have an eight o'clock meeting with Bonnie at her house. You know how she gets if I'm late, and it's pretty important, something to do with the exotic animal ordinance she's presenting at the council meeting….."

"Have you finally lost your mind? We have a murder here! One of my best reporters found the body. My paper will be the first to cover the story! Get your ass to the office," Alex shrieked. I held the phone away from my ear. Fred growled at it.

I kicked a tiny piece of driftwood out of my path as I kept walking.

"Geeze, Alex, can't Mid cover it? I mean, he's the crime reporter, right? I don't feel so great," I complained. This was not up my alley, a dead person. Since we haven't had much in the way of crime on Folly, I knew Mid would be all over this.

Alex sighed heavily. "Look, Kell, this is a unique situation we have here," she said. Why did I feel like I was two-years-old? "You found the body. You are covering this story. Besides, I couldn't find Mid now if I wanted to. He's in Myrtle Beach checking out the crab incident."

Ah, yes, I had forgotten. Someone was stealing blue crabs from traps from here to Myrtle Beach and Middleton was hot on the trail.

"Kell," she continued. "Go home, get dressed and come to work. I'll call Bonnie and reschedule for you. Now hurry!"

Fred met my eyes with a look of pity. I don't like to be ordered around, and this was the second time in the past thirty minutes. I grudgingly made my way over the dunes and walked home.

I live in the bottom half of a beautiful house, which means I get to live alone, which I love, yet have the convenience of a close-by neighbor directly upstairs. Ludmilla Dubrov is a 6'2" chiropractor of Russian descent with a strange son named Elbert. Elbert is thirteen and almost as large as his mother. He spends most of his time in the backyard setting little plastic army men on fire. Ludmilla finds this amusing, possibly because of her heritage. I find it disturbing.

"Good morning, babushka," she bellowed from the deck, shaking out a colorfully striped rug. "Have a good run? Elbert, put away the exacto knife and get ready for school."

"Hey, Ludmilla," I coughed as tiny particles descended upon me. "Sure, just fine. Got to get ready for work. See you later." Chief Stoney had been quite adamant when he said not to talk about the body. Ms. DeWinter was going to put her neck out, not me.

"Wait a second," Ludmilla instructed, draping the rug over her deck and leaning forward on the railing. She is a big woman in every sense of the word, and in her present position her ample bosom threatened to send her careening over the edge of the deck by force of gravity. I backed up a step, just in case.

"You'll be at the council meeting tonight when we discuss this animal nuisance problem we're having, I imagine," she said. "Well, I am going to bring up the suggestion that we do away with the raccoons on the island. One sliced his way through my back door screen and ate all of Gorby's cat food, then proceeded to relieve himself on my kitchen counter."

I studied her from below. Peroxide-blonde hair hung in ringlets around her scalp. She resembled an oversized Raggedy Ann doll with a dye job.

"The issue is about people keeping exotic animals on the islands as pets, Ludmilla, not about animals indigenous to Folly. Raccoons don't qualify as exotic," I explained.

She contemplated my response for a second, shrugged her broad shoulders and responded, "Fine, I'll just have Elbert handle the pests." She turned and went inside, slamming the door behind her.

I stood there for a moment and sighed. Elbert and I had finally come to terms on harassing the animal population. After all the years I'd spent living in other countries and observing just exactly what some people called food, I am foolishly tenderhearted. I don't even squish our state mascot, the palmetto bug, should I find one in the house. I simply shoo it outside.

Four years ago I was sunbathing in the backyard, marveling at the snowy white egrets in the marsh, when suddenly something whizzed by my head. Out of the giant oak tree close by an object fell to the ground with a light thump. Barely taking the time to tie my bikini top on, I ran to the spot and found a squirrel shot straight through the head. Horrified, I looked back towards the house. The then nine-year-old Elbert was up on the top deck, BB gun in hand, grinning with delight. Until, that is, I let out the scream of a banshee and raced up the steps, tackling him to the ground. He was shorter then, so with the adrenaline rush I didn't have much of a problem. His screams brought his mother running and even though I was hysterical she had no problem yanking me off her son. What followed was a passionate outpouring from me while Elbert swore they were tree rats. Just as I was about to pounce on him again, Ludmilla calmly declared a truce, no more squirrel shooting. Elbert argued, but finally listened after I threatened to get the mayor's wife involved. Faced with Ludmilla's snippy comment on the raccoons, I'd corner the kid and remind him I have friends in high places.

I retrieved my keys from their hiding spot beneath the potted hibiscus next to my front door and went inside. I filled Fred's water bowl, poured him some food and got out of the way just before he flopped down on my feet. Sampson practically growled with approval as I opened a rare can of cat food. Normally I stick with the dry variety, but I was feeling rather softhearted after the morning's excitement. I was sticky with sweat and the odd smell of fog mixed with something I couldn't name. Shower running, I checked to see what was clean, pulled out my favorite slouchy capris with the side pockets for my gear and a white cotton tank top. Jumping in the shower, I let the hot water steam away memories of the morning.

The smell of raspberry scented shampoo enveloped me. Eyes closed, I saw the dead girl's face. She looked surprised. Did she know her killer? Did she struggle? Who were her parents? Did she have a boyfriend? Or a dog? I felt sick to my stomach and opened my eyes.

Dressed, I grabbed my purse and big black carryall that held my notebooks, pens, pencils, address book, water bottle and mace. "See you later, buddy." I scratched Fred behind the ears. He was snoring. I envied him.

Locking the door behind me, I turned and jumped. "Shit, Elbie, you startled me," I said to my neighbor. Elbert was right outside my front door. I held my hand up to shield my eyes from the sun as I looked at him. His dusky brown hair was as unkempt as usual and I spotted a few new pimples sprouting on his puberty-stricken face.

"Hi, Kell. Guess who's coming to visit? Mean ol' motherfuckin' Murphy," he said, following me to my car.

"Don't swear, Elbie, you're too young. I didn't know your mom still kept in touch with him," I said, unlocking the door to my red Toyota Four Runner.

Murphy is Ludmilla's sometime boyfriend. He hasn't lived with her since I've been here, but does visit occasionally. They have a disturbingly volatile relationship, and Elbert does not help the cause. Time to stay away from home.

"When is he coming?"

"Dunno, but I don't like it. Maybe one of your police friends can lock him up or something," he suggested. I knew he was not joking.

"Listen, Elbie, I have to get to the paper. I'm sure it will all work out," I said, starting the car and rolling down my window.

My six-foot something young neighbor had a deserted expression on his face. He picked a scab on his arm. "It'd better work out. I got an exacto knife and I ain't afraid to use it."

I put my car in gear, left one alarming arena and made my way to another.

CHAPTER FOUR

L ike I said, Folly is a mere six-mile stretch of land from one point to the other. I live on the east end, close to the old Coast Guard station and the Morris Island lighthouse. As I made my way from home, visions of a maniacal Elbert dancing in my already cluttered head, I approached the area referred to as "the washout". The stretch of beach has the statewide reputation for producing the best waves, so naturally it's where the surfers hang out. Normally, I fly by at record speed, dodging open car doors, bike-riding kids with surfboards under their arms and forty-something men on skateboards. Under the circumstances, I slowed to a crawl.

A group of five or six guys stood on the side of the road, leaning against cars and staring out at the sea. Not a head turned as I puttered by. Hmm. A little further down a young woman balanced a rather long board on her head, making her way to the water. I wondered if she knew the dead girl. "NO KOOKS" was spray painted on one of the large rocks barricading the washout. I glanced around guiltily, certain I would be pegged as a kook if caught dilly-dallying.

At Center Street, the main drag in my tiny town, I waited for the light to change. I glanced longingly at the Coast, a favorite gathering place. They don't serve coffee, but no problem because I felt in strange need of a beer. Or something stronger. This, I sighed, was going to be a long day.

Passing City Hall and the police station, I resisted the urge to put it in park and stroll in, casually asking if anything new was happening. Chief Stoney had looked pretty mad. I parked my Four Runner out front of *The Archipelago's* headquarters a few blocks up the road and took inventory. My editor's black Saab was of course here. I spotted vehicles belonging to our receptionist, sportswriter, food section reporter, James Island reporter and a couple of the photographers. Mid's shiny red 1969 Mustang convertible was noticeably absent, he still searching for the crab thief.

"Hey, Myra, how're you this fine morning," I greeted our receptionist, attempting to sound like my usual cheerful self.

"I do believe they are waiting for you, Kell. Mr. Lyons arrived at eight o'clock sharp," Myra Glass replied. She's about 65 years old and a former school reporter. "Would you like a cup of coffee," she asked, standing and smoothing her modest camel colored skirt and ignoring my open mouth.

"Mr. Lyons is here? Why? Where's he at." I tried to use Myra for cover as I peered into the newsroom.

"Here, dear, take the coffee, there you go. Now, there's nothing to worry about, Mr. Lyons does check in from time to time," Myra soothed. "His is the publisher, after all."

I reached for the coffee and looked behind her again. There. In Alex's office. I could see through the glass enclosure the two of them scheming something up which undoubtedly concerned the dead girl, and quite possibly me.

"Myra, let me use your phone real quick," I held out my hand for the device, frantically punching in numbers. "Answer, answer, answer," I pleaded.

Yes! The sound of the line picking up was replaced by a thud and some unintelligible cursing. A few seconds later "What?" came through loud and clear, although a bit on the mean side.

"Mid, it's me. Listen, there are some freaking hairy things going on here and you need to come home, I -------"

"Kell! Can't you see I'm trying to sleep here," my dear friend and co-reporter interrupted. "I've been up all night in the middle of the ocean lying in wait for a damn crab thief with a crabber named Bubba, who doesn't smell as if he'd bathed in the last century, just so you know, and his equally smelly and toothless wife. I am not in the mood to talk to you. Good-bye."

"Wait, Mid, I don't want to cover this one! Mid? Middleton Langdon Calhoun, don't you hang up on me," I hollered in to the mouth piece. The line was dead. He had hung up on me. Son-of-a-bitch. I will never cover for your sorry ass again, I thought. I also wondered why there were so many people around here named Bubba.

"Really, Kell, you've nothing to fear from Mr. Lyons. He's really quite a pussycat," said Myra, her bifocals perched on the end of her nose.

I stared at her. Mr. Lyons is really a gentle kitty cat, not a lion after all. Right. I peeked in his direction again. From my vantage point, he actually resembled a door. At 6'7" and 350 pounds, Emmet Lyons had spent the better part of his life as an offensive lineman for the New York Giants, keeping equally angry, large men from hurting his quarterback. A native New Yorker, his impressive size works to his advantage down here in the good old south. The rednecks generally think twice before telling him where to stick his Yankee attitude.

Myra patted me on the back, nudging me in the direction of my desk. It's right next to Mid's and across from Holly Chesnut's, the food section writer. Next to her is our entertainment reporter, Kevin Prentiss, the only married one among us, who has a wife and three kids. The other desks line up in two rows, culminating at the glass enclosure housing Ms. DeWinter and, presently, Mr. Lyons.

"Oh, Kell, Alex told us about how you found the body. My gosh, aren't you simply grossed out," whispered Holly in a ladylike southern drawl. "I mean, I don't know how I'm ever going to write about food today, I'm like, so grossed out." Her perfectly polished fingertips massaged her forehead in perfectly uniformed circles. Alex adores her. For the life of me, I don't see why.

"Well, Holly, let's see? Grossed out? Nah, it's real life drama here. Terribly sad, of course, but Mid's gonna love this one."

Holly leaned back in her chair. She fluffed her naturally curly auburn hair around her shoulders and leaned forward. "Oh but no, I overheard them talking," she gestured towards Alex's office, red tips fluttering. "We're having a staff meeting soon, and I think you're going to handle this one, Kell."

I flopped my bag down on my desk, searching for a clear spot. "Huh, you're kidding. Well, Holly, I don't want to talk about this anymore. Why don't you go do whatever it is you do here." Okay, I was being bitchy, but Holly always made me bitchy and this was bitchiness in overdrive. She stomped off in the direction of the bathrooms.

I reached for my phone to retrieve my messages, glancing to see if I'd been spotted yet. Nope, they were still huddled together. Maybe Mr. Lyons was reliving his days in football. Good, I thought, maybe this is a long and complicated play they're discussing.

I had fourteen new messages, five of which were from Bonnie McLeod. Alex had not divulged the severity of the morning, and Bonnie was pretty peeved at being put on the back burner. Her last message ended with "the boa constrictor is still loose on the island and Henry Matson's Chihuahua is missing." Tonight's Town Council meeting was going to be a doozie. All of the island would turn out to debate over the implementation of a law prohibiting "exotic animals" on Folly. I could hardly wait.

Before I could return any calls, Alex and Mr. Lyons emerged from her office. My smart and savvy editor made a beeline for my desk, heels clicking and eyes focused. On me.

"You are here," she observed. Mr. Lyons loomed in the background, casting a rather shadow over her.

"Yep, just trying to return some calls. Hey, Mr. Lyons, how's it going," I offered a friendly, albeit contrived, greeting. I tried to look busy by shuffling papers around my desk.

He cleared his throat. It sounded like a growl. "You made a very important discovery this morning, Ms. Palevac."

"Oh, really, it was nothing, all in a day's work, as they say. Someone had to do it, right?" I chuckled. Alex and Mr. Lyons simply stared at me like I had ten heads.

"Kell, we were going to wait and have a staff meeting to discuss this, but it really is unnecessary. Mr. Lyons and I have decided since you made the discovery, and since you are the reporter for the City of Folly Beach, you will be covering this story." Alex gave me that fixed glare I knew meant to keep my mouth shut.

My mouth opened on its own. I glanced at Mr. Lyons. It closed again.

"Therefore," Alex continued, "You will be dealing with Chief Stoney and the rest of the officers involved. I have already called him to inform him of this, and he will be most cooperative.

Yeah, right.

"They have identified the body and are notifying next of kin. We are allowed to talk to the chief to get a brief statement for tomorrow's paper," my editor said. "From there, you will be handling all follow ups."

Mr. Lyons placed a large mitt on my shoulder. His eyes actually looked kind and sympathetic. "You are an excellent reporter, Ms. Palevac. We have the utmost confidence in your ability to handle this."

Damn if I didn't preen. Really, all of this praise from the publisher was going straight to my head. I opened my mouth.

"Well, sir, I'll do my best. You know, maybe I'm up for this after all. I mean, what's a dead body in the scheme of things, right? Could be a whole lot worse. Could be several dead bodies, right? Sure, I can handle this, no problemo."

They looked at each other, then back at me in unison. I swear two sets of eyebrows raised on cue.

"We are certain that you can," Alex said. One large and one small body did an about face and marched back to the direction from which they came.

CHAPTER FIVE

The everyday noises of the newsroom were getting on my nerves. Joelle and Reid, the two photographers hanging around at the moment, were blissfully engaged in a game of cards. No dead body for them. Holly had returned from her sulking episode and was sneaking looks at me from beneath hooded eyelids. The police scanner positioned near Mid's desk went off every so often. I resisted the urge to throw my coffee cup at it.

Two desks down Kenneth Linski, our sportswriter, was pecking away feverishly at his computer. Lean, tanned arms emerged from a faded t-shirt that looked to be about two sizes too small. His spiky yellow hair sprouted up, clumped in sections where he pulled at it. Round wire-rimmed glasses reflected light from the screen. I knew he was attempting to wrap up an article from last night's James Island High School soccer game.

"Pretty cool about your dead girl, Kell," he said, fingers flying over his keyboard. "Some people have all the luck."

I looked at my coffee cup, contemplating the indentation it would make in his skull. "She's not my dead girl, you moron, I probably wouldn't have even seen her if it wasn't for Fred. He found her."

Holly smirked, tossed her head, and gave Kenneth a loving glance. Two peas in a pod, I thought. When Kenneth had first started here I had fixed him with a glance like that myself, until I met his German boyfriend named Hans. Evidently, Holly and Kenneth had been born with the identical shopping gene and quickly became best of friends. They often hit the stores together in their down time, dragging a disgruntled Hans in tow.

"Actually, you know, this might be interesting," I said. I lowered my voice. "Do you guys realize this is the first murder here since the Granger case?"

Holly leaned forward, blue eyes round as saucers. Kenneth stopped typing.

"Yep," I continued, "Junior Granger was a drifter here back in the early seventies. He lured three teenagers into an empty vacation house on East Erie, raped them and cut them up in little bitty pieces. Took eons to put them all back together again."

Holly looked strangely pale, which was comforting. Kenneth gave a snort.

"We've all heard about that case, Palevac. This isn't going to be such a big deal."

He returned to his pecking.

"Oh really? What makes you say that, Linski? When was the last time you found anybody dead around here?"

Kenneth twirled around in his chair to face me. "Seriously, folks, this is a surfer here. Come on, she probably kicked it from doing one too many bong hits. Everyone knows the only things surfers do is get high, ride waves, sleep and get high again." He turned back to his computer, dragging a spiked section of hair straight up. "Shit, they probably don't even take time to eat, they're all so fuckin' skinny."

My coffee cup missed him by inches, crashing onto the floor. Okay, so I was aiming for his foot instead of his head in a moment of sanity. Holly squeaked. I was on my feet in a flash.

"You," I screamed, "are a simple-minded, stereotypical thinking imbecile with the sensitivity of a baboon. You are an impediment to society!" My hands splayed on his desk as I tried not to hyperventilate. Holly squeaked again.

Kenneth didn't move. He actually looked afraid behind his wire frames, eyes shifting for some safe spot to focus on. They found a point behind me.

I felt a tap on my shoulder. "What?" I barked, whirling around. Alex DeWinter stood ramrod straight, arms folded across her midsection. Her sky blue jacket matched the icy blue of her eyes. I wondered how she kept her hair from moving. Unfolding her arms, she glanced at the three of us. Holly returned the look, apparently confident she was not in any trouble here. Kenneth tried to speak, but was sliced to silence.

"Children, if I could I would put you all in time out. You're very fortunate Mr. Lyons has already left, or you would be going to the principal's office to explain yourselves. I, however, have more important things to do than listen to your paltry explanations as to why you can't get along." With that Alex spun on her spiked heel.

While Kenneth and I glared at each other, Holly made little clucking noises and shook her head. The phone rang.

I snatched it up before anyone else. "Newsroom," I snarled. A heavily accented male voice announced himself.

"Hold on a minute," I said. "Hey lover boy, your Weiner schnitzel is yodeling for you."

Kenneth picked up his phone and covered the mouthpiece. "Fuck you, Palevac."

"Sorry, jackass, you wouldn't know what to do with the equipment."

I grabbed my bag and made a high speed exit.

CHAPTER SIX

Myra Glass was busily opening mail as I stomped by her desk on my way out. She kept at her task, although she had heard every word. "Have a nice day, dear," she sang out. I grunted an unintelligible response. I'd make it up to her. Maybe I'd buy her a plant.

"That little wanna-be sports writer, I should kick his ass just for shits and giggles, how dare he trivialize my dead girl, he's really asking for it this time, Hans or no Hans, I'll aim at his empty head next time.........." I was fuming as I left the building. Hands in my pockets and head down, I plowed into someone. Objects hit the pavement. Long reddish hair swirled in my line of vision as my feet got tangled with two others and we went down.

Green cat eyes flared. "For the love of God, Kell, what are you doin'? If you want to rumble, just say so." Siobhan Mulvaney hoisted herself up from the ground, pulling me with her.

"Crap, Siobhan, I'm sorry. Are you all right?" I asked.

"Sure, sure, Kell, but the question is, are you all right." Siobhan pushed her hair out of her face. "I could hear you up the road, you sound like you're fighting the Christian invasion of Ireland. What's up?"

I brushed myself off while Siobhan did the same. "Nothing," I said.

"Nothing? Nothing, she says! You look as mad as one of

my ancestors, riding to battle with nothing on but war paint," she exclaimed, eyes dancing.

Siobhan can trace her heritage back to the days of the Celts invading Rome around the time of 226 BC, a point which she and my mother can spend hours on end discussing. She is also my best friend, besides Mid.

"Seriously, I'm sorry for knocking you over. It's just that Linski in there really ticked me off. I shouldn't let him get to me like that."

"Linski? You're letting the likes of him get to you? Please, woman, you have more upstairs than that, doncha? And by the way, I took pictures of your dead girl earlier," she said. "Alex wants a shot for tomorrow's edition, but I don't know if Lyons will run it."

"Oh for heaven's sake, she is not my dead girl, this is getting completely out of hand," I paused. "I didn't know Alex had asked for photos." Siobhan is one of our four photographers, and I might add, our best.

She looked at me, hands on her hips, juggling two camera bags and a backpack around her shoulders. At five foot-seven, Siobhan dwarfs me by a good three inches. Peering closer, she scrutinized my face.

"You look like shit, darlin'. Where'ya headed?"

Always trust a true friend to tell you the truth. "I was going to see if the chief had a minute," I said.

Siobhan swung her bags onto one arm and linked the other through mine. "Let's go then. All that little man gets is a minute though. After that, you're buying me breakfast."

We walked towards City Hall, which serves as the police station and fire station. Most of the locals were either already up and off to work, or still asleep. We have a pretty diverse group of residents on Folly. I tend to categorize them into the daytime folks and the nighttime folks, as some don't open an eye until at least mid-afternoon. At this hour, the streets were fairly empty.

"My, someone's up early," Siobhan commented, watching a straggly haired man dressed in faded jeans and flip flops cross the road. "Top of the mornin' to ya, Hatch! Where are you headed on this fine morning?"

He stopped and squinted at us. "Home to bed." Hatch walked our way. "Been up all night shooting pool at the Coast." He reached in a pocket and pulled out a handful of crumpled bills. "Won, too," he said and grinned. A loud belch emerged from somewhere deep within his lanky body. "Too much beer," he muttered. His blood-shot eyes gave us the once over. "You two want to come over and hang out awhile? There's a six pack of Rolling Rock in my fridge."

Siobhan tilted her head to one side and gave me a questioning look, an impish grin lighting up her eyes. "What'cha say, Kell? Might be just what you need to forget your troubles?"

The old saying "when Irish eyes are smiling they're usually up to something" is a fine handle to hang on my always ready for fun friend. Actually, after the morning I'd had it wouldn't take much to sway me from my stoic work ethic. Echoes of my grandfather's advice kept me from folding. Gustave Palevac emigrated with his parents from Czechoslovakia to the United State as a young boy and I cherished the times we visited him. "Work hard, Kell, it is the price of success," he would tell me. He died two years ago and I miss him constantly. Thanks, Gramps, I thought. I met Siobhan's eyes and shook my head.

"Thanks, Hatch, but we've got work to do. See you at the council meeting tonight," I said, steering Siobhan around him.

We watched him sway towards home. "At least you don't have to drive around Folly to get where you're going, for the most part," I said. "Can't see the harm in walking home after a few too many."

Siobhan chuckled. "Unless they all started bumping into each other on the streets. Remember when they found Scary Harry sleeping on the front steps of St. John's?"

That had caused quite a scene on a beautiful Sunday morning at the Catholic church. Apparently, several of the church elders had arrived before the 8 a.m. service and discovered Scary Harry spread out like an offering on the stairs. He got his nickname because he'd deserved it. He wore an eye patch, said to have lost the eye in a fight involving a fish hook. On that fateful morning his patch was missing and the church elders were faced with a one-eyed man who resembled a bulldog.

"Poor Mrs. Gaillard has never been the same," I said. "Her husband says she still wakes up screaming about the devil on the church steps." One thing we aren't lacking on Folly Beach is our share of excitement, however tame. We laughed. I felt much better by the time we arrived at City Hall.

We entered the three-story pale-peach stucco building and climbed the steps. I waved at Marjorie Tolle, Director of Public Information, and made my way down the hall to the station.

Connie Albright, the police dispatcher on duty, brightened when she saw us. "Hey girls, we got us a little action today, don't we? I can't remember when this place was so busy." Her short brown hair bobbed up and down, keeping time with her mouth. "Chief and the boys, they've been talking all morning with the coroner and all sorts of important people, don't know who for sure, but they sound important." The phone rang. "Hold on a minute. Folly Beach police station. Oh, hi, Mr. Hennessey. Snowpuff's stuck in the tree again? I'll send Officer

Bresseau. Well, I don't know if the boa constrictor was caught yet."

She glanced at us, saw us shaking our heads. "Well, that's a negative, Mr. Hennessey, but I'm sure Snowpuff won't come to no harm up in the tree. Yes, of course I'll send an officer." She hung up and punched a number. "Bresseau, go to the Hennessey place and bring a ladder. Now, where were we?"

I cleared my throat. "Connie, can you see if the chief has a minute?"

Connie looked excited, Siobhan looked impatient and I probably looked doomed. A buzzer rang, and we were admitted. Pushing open the entranceway, I heard the hum of voices behind closed doors.

"Chief Stoney, Kell Palevac is here to see you, sir," Connie announced loudly through the intercom.

"Does she have an appointment?" his booming voice demanded. Connie glanced at me expectantly. "Do you have an appointment?" she asked hopefully.

"Tell him she only has a minute to spare and he better hurry it up," my Celtic warrior companion disguised as my friend responded. She held a camera bag in front of her like a shield.

"No, stop," I peeped as Connie began to press the intercom button." Tell him this will only take a minute. My editor sent me."

Connie looked at Siobhan with something akin to admiration. She shrugged her shoulders. "She says her editor sent her and it will only take a minute."

I glanced around the room as the silence threatened to continue indefinitely. Siobhan began whistling an Irish jig, hopping from one foot to the other. "Would you stop?" I was testy. She stuck her tongue out at me.

"Send her in," the chief said. Connie sighed happily and motioned us to the first closed door on the right. "Folly Beach police station" we heard her answer the ringing phone as Siobhan turned the doorknob. She pushed me through the open door, right into the path of Chief Stoney's desk.

He was smoking a cigarette, feet on his desk, watching the haze rise to the ceiling. The head of a buck was mounted to the wall directly behind him. Scanning the room, I saw a fox, a boar and several colorful fish. Now I remembered why he and Bonnie McLeod had issues.

"Ladies, have a seat." Chief Stoney snubbed out his cigarette and reached into his shirt pocket for another. "Ms. Mulvaney, I wasn't expecting you. How do I look?"

Siobhan narrowed her eyes. "I'm along for the ride, Chief, not to make your portrait."

"Chief," I quickly interjected. "Ms. DeWinter said I could expect a brief statement concerning the, uh, discovery this morning." I whipped out my notebook. Pen poised, I waited.

He brought his legs down from his desktop, inhaled deeply, and blew out a stream of smoke. Inhaling again, he blew smoke rings towards the light bulb above his head. Chief Stoney kept this up until one ring encircled the fixture perfectly. One hand laid upon the desk, he tapped out a steady beat. I looked at the stuffed boar's head. That was one sketchy looking creature. Just as I was beginning to get lost in thought, contemplating the last moments of the poor mahi-mahi attached to the wall, mouth gaping in obvious surprise, he spoke.

"Ms. Palevac, it is an irony that you discovered the first murder on Folly Beach in three decades, and I do appreciate your sensitivity to the subject, being a woman and all." Siobhan opened her mouth and I kicked her. "We have identified the young woman as a Jennifer Donnelly, age 19, a student at the

College of Charleston. Her roommate reported her missing yesterday after she failed to return from a day at the beach."

I scribbled quickly. "Had anyone been looking for her since that time?"

Chief Stoney sighed. "It hadn't even been twenty-four hours yet, and usually these kids turn up safe and sound." He put out his cigarette and reached for another. "Anyone care for a cigarette?"

I kicked Siobhan again before she could respond. She had promised to quit and this really didn't seem too professional anyways. "No, sir, thank-you all the same. Where was she from?"

"Inland a ways, near Florence. Her parents are on their way to identify the body, although her roommate has already done that. Ah, man, they are so torn up." He stared at the smoke rings circling his head.

"Do we have any suspects, or anything to go on at this juncture?" I asked.

"It's too soon, Kell. Just report the details. She died of strangulation sometime last night between nine p.m. and midnight, according to Coroner Hagood. She was a good student, a well-liked person on campus, and had several surfing friends," he said.

I made a mental note to check out these surfing friends. "Who is handling the investigation now?"

"We have the whole force questioning friends, the school faculty, anyone who might have known where Ms. Donnelly was yesterday," Chief Stoney replied, courteously blowing smoke away from my face. "We have extra patrol cars out right now, just checking on everything, making sure things appear to be operating routinely."

My pen paused in mid-stroke. My town is not know for its

run-of-the-mill functioning. It's nothing to see rowdy groups dancing in the streets till dawn, or mud wrestling in the empty lot on the corner by the Coast. Nobody but the cops blink when tourists go the wrong way down our one way street. We're so used to it we just swerve around them, although someone did paint a giant red arrow pointing in the right direction on the pavement a few months back. How exactly were we to determine if we were operating with all cells firing? Let's see, Mazo's Market was probably hopping by now, construction workers mixed with lawyers, doctors, landscapers and surfers all vying for a spot to pay for their morning coffees and papers. Or beers. I know them all fairly well. Maybe not all, but I have a good grasp of our scene. I knew the chief did, too. At least I prayed he did, now that we had an apparent killer in our midst.

"Well, now," Siobhan jumped up and clapped her hands twice. "I think we're about wrapped up here. Chief Stoney, we thank you so kindly for your hospitality. Say good-bye, Kell." She turned to the chief. "Ms. Palevac will be at your disposal throughout the day if you remember something you forgot, Chief."

He looked at her with a sincerely puzzled expression. Strom Stoney has been our chief of police for over twenty years and had handled everything from Hurricane Hugo to the daunting beach renourishment project orchestrated by the Army Corps of Engineers. I had never seen him at such a loss for words.

He put out his cigarette and pulled another out of the pack in his shirt pocket. The poor chief was really stressed, and for the first time in all my years of dealing with him I felt a touch of compassion.

I rummaged through my bag and found a card, handed it to him and said, "Thanks for your time, Chief Stoney. Please call me with any more news on this case." I figured the card was on its way to the trash can before we had made it out the door, but, hey, I knew where to find him.

We waved good-bye to Connie, who was deep in conversation. "Hold on a minute, Martha. See you again soon, girls." She grinned. Connie had most likely already hit the airwaves about the murder, and news spreads like wildfire in this little beach town. So much for a scoop on the story, I thought. We made for the streets.

CHAPTER SEVEN

So, girl, where are we eating? How about the Starfish?" Siobhan asked. "I'm so hungry I could eat a horse. Which reminds me, did I tell you about that funky restaurant they closed down yesterday?"

We walked across the street and made our way to the Starfish. Ah, yes, I remembered the case of the suspicious eatery Holly had been working on. She had gone to do a review of the new dining establishment and saw a car leaving from the employee entrance with a bumper sticker that read I like cats, they taste like chicken.

"I thought Holly was just being her usual paranoid self," I said. "You mean that thing checked out?"

"Yep, after Holly reported her misgivings to DHEC, they showed up with a search warrant. Found the whole hindquarters of a dog in the freezer, among other tasty treats." Siobhan laughed.

I stopped short. "You are kidding me! Tell me you're lying, Siobhan." I really didn't feel like eating anymore.

"Nope, it's the truth, it will be in tomorrow's paper if that airhead finishes her article. I got some great shots of the place emptying out, the employees were running like ants," she said.

I mulled this over in my head, wondering what Bonnie McLeod would say when she read the article. She'd probably be trying to pass an amendment soon to keep all restaurateurs off Folly.

We walked into the Starfish and made our way to a booth by the window. The Starfish is right on the corner of Center Street and Ashley Avenue, making for a great people watching spot. It's also one of the only places to eat in town where you walk in with just a bathing suit on if the mood strikes you. The atmosphere is beachy, with shades of turquoise sponge-painted on the walls, large potted plants and shells everywhere, both painted versions artfully framed and real ones scattered around the restaurant.

"Hi, y'all," greeted Sue, one of the waitresses on duty today. Short and round, she's a well-made testimony to the tasty vittles the Starfish dishes up. She pulled a pencil out of her ponytail. "What'll it be?"

Siobhan straightened in her seat. "Two eggs over easy, wheat toast, grits and hash browns and crispy bacon. Oh, and milk and orange juice," she said. "I'm so hungry I could eat----"

"I know, I know, keep it to yourself, okay," I interrupted. She can be so annoying sometimes. Frowning, I asked for a bowl of cheerios.

"That's it? How can you exist on a bowl of cereal, Kell? Order some breakfast," Siobhan commanded.

"I'm not hungry anymore, that's all I want."

"Get her what I'm having, Sue, the poor dear's havin' a rough morning, she's not right in the head."

"Stop it, Siobhan, I don't want anything else."

"You've got to eat some food, at least have a little bacon or something. Sue, bring her some bacon."

"No! I just want cheerios."

Sue looked back and forth between us, apparently undecided as to who was in charge of my breakfast.

"Fine, fine, starve if you want to. Let her starve, Sue, just bring her the cheerios." Siobhan sighed dramatically.

Sue gave me a weak little smile and ambled off in the direction of the kitchen. Siobhan made a face at me, retrieved her sunglasses from atop her head and put them on. Incognito now, she rested her chin in her hands and stared out the window at unsuspecting passersby. Normally, I do the same, but today I looked around the room checking out our dining partners.

I recognized several, including Judge Preston Brooks, who I've had the pleasure of appearing before concerning one or two, okay, a few speeding tickets. In his fifties, he's bald except for a graying ponytail at the nape of his neck. He suffers from somewhat of a Napoleon complex, usually wearing elevated shoes to give him a boost.

When I first moved on to Folly fresh out of college, I made the mistake of arguing with him in court one time and had been severely reprimanded and severely fined to boot. Lesson learned. Don't ever piss off a judge in a town the size of mine, even if you know you're right.

An officer had pulled me over for an expired registration sticker on my license plate. At our court hearing I put up such a stink about the unfairness of the fine involved and so flustered the poor officer that he spit out "exposed resurrection" when addressing Judge Brooks. The others in the courtroom had laughed hysterically and the judge had to order silence. Thus, I'd made an enemy for life. Today, said enemy was polishing off a stack of pancakes when he glanced up and noticed me looking at him. I tried a slight smile and was rewarded with a glare. Screw him, I thought, and glared right back. I also made a mental note to keep an eye on my speedometer.

To my right sat Delores Ditalli and her much younger significant other, Lou Rinaldi. They're New Jersey transplants who've lived here longer than I have. Delores is of an indeterminable age, with deeply tanned skin, platinum hair and lots of plastic surgery. I squinted at her. Yep, her face looked even tighter that the last time I saw her. She had on so much jewelry she sparkled. Lou is about forty-five, sports a full head of slicked back, inky black hair and impressive biceps bulging out of his too tight shirt. Rumor has it they orchestrate the largest drug ring on the island, but, hey, I'm not reporting on it. Delores flashed me a toothy smile and Lou hefted a large forearm in my direction.

At the counter sat three youngish looking men. Guy number one wore faded jeans, Reef sandals, a tattered t-shirt with Rip Curl across the back and a beanie pulled low on his head. In the middle, number two wore baggy long shorts, nondescript sandals, a sweatshirt that said tavi...heavy soul, and a beanie which barely contained a mass of dreadlocks. On the end, guy number three sported greenish cargo style pants and, surprise, a beanie. No shirt or shoes in sight. He was holding a copy of today's paper and his lips moved while he read. Surfers.

Unabashedly eavesdropping, I strained to hear what this sort talks about.

Guy number one: Dude, did you catch that swell last night? They were peeling left and sooooo narly, I did a giant floater, came off the lip and smacked it so hard. Whoosh, smack, kapow." Accompanied by hand gestures.

Guy number two: Fuckin' A I caught it. I dropped in on old man Cheves, that freakin' lawyer, it was totally awesome. Old longboardin' fart said he was gonna sue me." Accompanied by laughter.

Guy number three: "Hey Harley, what does this word mean, a-t-r-o-p-h-i-e-d?"

Accompanied by a puzzled expression.

Number one leaned across number two and looked at the paper in number three's hands. "Atrophied, like in what happens to your dick on cold days in the water, man."

The lights came on in number three's head. "Oh, yeah, that really sucks."

So much for what this sort talks about, I thought. Siobhan came out of her trance and caught me looking at the trio. She raised her shades, eyes shrewd and wiggled her eyebrows at me. "Remembering the good ol' days with Fletcher?"

I scoffed at her. "Get real, that was in college for crying out loud. Way ancient history, you know that." Fletcher was a guy I dated for awhile, a surfer type who had a commitment problem. He was totally, unequivocally committed to surfing, while our relationship went something like this: Me waiting to be picked up to go to lunch, him calling from the beach saying, hey, the waves are hittin', you understand, right? Right. Last I heard he was out in California somewhere. He did, however, expose me a bit to the surfing world during our rocky romance, which might come in handy considering the current situation. I had a sudden recollection that Preston Brooks had been one of the surfers always in the water.

Our food arrived and Siobhan got busy. I pushed my cheerios around in their bowl, sinking them and thinking about what else some people eat that we don't. I remembered how when we lived in Brasil and one of my cats disappeared and my brother and I made signs and posted them everywhere, hoping someone would find Georgie and return him. Our maid, Carminha, just kept making tsk tsk sounds and shaking her head. A few days later, she was on the phone talking to her sister, telling her how the *"favela",* or street children, had taken my cat for dinner. Infuriated, Aidan and I rode our bikes down the steep hill we lived on and ventured into the land of the favelas, where we weren't allowed to go. Thirteen at the time, Aidan rode right up to a group of street urchins like a mighty warrior, demanding in his fluent Portuguese that they return Georgie. Laughing, their brown skin dirty and their brown eyes mocking, they rubbed their bellies and made burping noises. I grabbed a handful of rocks and pelted them, screaming all the obscenities I had ever heard in my eleven years. Angry now, they started to come after us, but Aidan and I had the advantage of bicycles and left them shouting in our wake.

I pushed my now soggy bowl of cereal away from me just as the doors to the restaurant burst open, two highly agitated young women spilling inside. Both tan, with hair streaked from the sun, I recognized them as renters of one of the apartments above the Starfish. The one with short hair had on a long t-shirt and slippers and the other had on a red plaid robe. It didn't take a reporter to notice it looked like they had just stumbled out of bed.

"Mikey, Harley, oh no, oh no," sobbed one, flinging herself into the midst of the three at the counter. "She's dead, Jenny's dead!"

Before the other one could launch herself at the group, guys number one, two and three stood up, catching hold of an arm here and a shoulder there. "What? Quit crying, Alana, settle down, who's dead? What are you talkin' about?" asked number two.

"Oh, Creech, she's really dead, Jenny was murdered! Some girl jogging on the beach found her this morning," red plaid robe wailed, clinging to her friends. I slunk down in my seat.

By now the entire restaurant was abuzz with the news, the five surfers the center of attention as other patrons, Sue, the cook and the busboy all gathered around them. Apparently, the two girls had been peacefully sleeping just minutes before, probably dreaming of the waves of the previous night, only to be awakened by the ring of their telephone and the bearer of bad news.

Siobhan finished off the last of her grits. "Well, knew it was only a matter of time before all this got out. I'm stuffed, you ready to go?"

I shushed her. "Hold on, I'm trying to listen here, this is my story, you know." Really, Siobhan still had no clue when it came to reporting.

She threw up her hands. "Why don't you just go introduce yourself to them, tell them you found her, ask your questions. Come on, I'll handle it."

"I will squish you like a bug if you so much as move."

Siobhan crossed her arms over her chest and slumped down in her seat so we were now on eye level. "Reporters," she mumbled.

My fiery red-headed friend does not understand you don't go barreling like a kid in a candy store towards your target to obtain sensitive information. Not that I had ever been faced with a murder before, but there was a bit of tact required. I listened.

I gleaned from the nature of the many people talking at once that Jennifer Donnelly had been a close friend of the group, which was now gathering themselves for a hasty exit. "I've gotta get dressed, let's go back upstairs," said short hair. Heads shaking, somber expressions and babbling voices left together. "We'll find out who did this, don't you worry, Jenny," vowed guy number two, pulling off his beanie and letting a jumble of long brown dreadlocks loose.

Jennifer Donnelly, who was currently lying naked on a cold metal table in the morgue, was surely not worried. I, on the other hand, got a chill up my spine when I felt Judge

Brooks' eyes boring in on me as he slapped money down on his table, pausing when he passed our booth.

Up close he resembled a scrawny ferret, with yellowing teeth and beady brown eyes. The light above our table reflected off the top of his skull as he leaned forward.

"Just one less fool to deal with out in the line up," he hissed. His putrid breath made me lean far, far back in my seat. For once I had absolutely nothing to say. Siobhan, on the other hand, never seems to have that problem.

"So, Judge Brooks, sir, have you decided what to do with your, um, property?" she asked, meeting his sudden crazed expression with unabashed aplomb.

I sucked in my breath and kicked her under the table. Preston Brooks' property has been a bone of contention for the city for years, and just last month the Planning and Zoning Committee had once again turned down his plea to rezone the place. Brooks uses the house as a rental, and has petitioned time and time again to have the place rezoned for multi-family usage so he can tear the house down and erect three-story townhouses. Like most coastal towns, development is a huge issue on Folly, and I've witnessed some pretty ugly name calling at meetings involving the question to build or not to build. And, I might add, have reported gleefully when requests are denied. Hey, I don't want my little slice of heaven turned in to the next Myrtle Beach. I sank down in my seat.

Preston's face was now a rather odd shade of purple, his beady eyes bulging out bigger than I thought possible for beady eyes. The silence was marked by the sharp intake of his breath as he spoke.

"Well, Miz Mulvaney, Miz Palevac, perhaps justice will be served next time my petition makes it to the docket and you and your newspaper will be reportin' on my victory," he managed before swirling away in a haze of dark fury.

"Hmm, did I say something wrong?" Siobhan asked.

"Why did he have to include me in his answer, I didn't ask him the question, besides, why did you have to bring that up? Crap, I thought he hated me because of the ticket stuff. Now this too?" It really didn't seem like a great idea having the judge this ticked off at me. Forget the speedometer, maybe now I'd just never leave the house.

"Preston Brooks hates the world in general, so don't feel too special, darlin'," Siobhan retorted, standing up. "Let's go, we have a killer out there."

CHAPTER EIGHT

Back at my desk, I put the finishing touches on the short narrative describing the demise of the young surfer, trying to keep the image of Preston Brooks out of my head. I read it back to myself, knowing it sounded like a press release. I groaned at the end where I had written "further investigations are taking place into the apparent homicide", knowing full well who would be covering all the gory details. Now, before anyone cries wimp, I will defend myself by saying this is not what I normally write about.

I leaned back in my chair and let my head hang over the edge. The ceiling tiles were spotted with water stains and I amused myself shape-changing them into various animals. My emotions were haggling with each other and I was trying not to pay attention. In the Out box on my desk were two articles I had already completed.

See, I said to myself. A perfectly good story on the set of twins who were born deaf and had just received cochlear implants. Siobhan had come along with me on the interview to take photos, and their adorably cherubic faces were sure to set the article off just right. And this, right here, an expose on the fundraiser helping himself to the funds. This is what I write about, and damn well, too. Mine was the stuff of human interest, what Mid referred to as the "fluffy stuff". The phrase normally didn't bother me, but now, in the midst of the all too sobering, all too horrifying reality of Death, it sounded like a giant white marshmallow.

The sounds of the newsroom droned on, oblivious to my internal dilemma. I put my head to my desk, used my arms as a pillow, and listened. After so many years, I find the noises comforting and familiar and can zone out here practically at will. I watched as a fax came in, the steady stream of white paper folding over on itself. Phones jangled, chair legs scooted back on the linoleum floor, fingers danced over keyboards. The steady whir of the overhead fans created a hypnotic, endless pulse of motion and I felt my eyes flutter shut.

Cocooned in my safe half-sleep, I was vaguely aware of my co-workers as they came and went. Then I wasn't.

"Kell," someone whispered. "Kell, wake up." Then someone was shaking my shoulder. I didn't need to open my eyes to know who it was, because I smelled him, or rather his signature aftershave. I breathed deep, inhaling the clean citrusy aroma and opened one eye.

"Hi honey, I'm home," he said, smiling brightly. Middleton Calhoun sat perched on my desk, looking down at me with his warm brown eyes.

I closed my eye. Mid was here. Didn't I just talk to him in Myrtle Beach? What was he doing here?

"What are you doing here," I asked, sounding grumpy even to myself.

"Gee nice to see you, too. I almost killed myself on the highway getting back here so fast."

I kept my eyes closed. I didn't want to emerge from my state of unconsciousness, not even to talk to Mid. Especially not to talk to Mid, I remembered, as our brief telephone conversation of a few hours earlier sprang to mind.

"You hung up on me," I said.

"You woke me up," Mid said.

"It was an emergency."

"You always have emergencies, Kell. Besides, I'm here, aren't I?"

"A little late," I said.

"Late for what? I wasn't supposed to be here today. And will you open your eyes, damnit."

"Don't take that tone with me," I said, opening my eyes and balancing my chin on my hands.

We glared at each other. During this exchange I took in the details of my sparring partner. Brown tousled hair mixed with a little gray around the edges, deeply tanned skin, probably from days at sea with the crabbers, impeccably ironed tan linen shirt tucked into worn jeans. Black Costa Del Mar sunglasses perched on top of his head. Even while glaring he managed to look serenely calm, and perfectly immaculate, as usual.

The product of one of Charleston's oldest and most illustrious families, Middleton radiates the confidence and demeanor of a true Southern gentleman. And if I was honest with myself, I must admit he had been coming to my rescue since I was twelve. His parents had shipped him off to explore the world during his school years, and one year he simply appeared at the school Aidan and I attended in Rio de Janeiro. Mid's twenty-nine, almost thirty, same as my brother. He and Aidan became fast friends, with me tagging along to the various soccer games and other activities they participated in. As a reckless tomboy, I had gotten in to my share of scuffles with not only many an opposing team's player, but also boys who thought that by around age fourteen I should be noticing them. Mid was essentially an adopted brother, and the reason I'd applied to the College of Charleston in the first place.

He studied me. "You look like shit, Kell."

What was this? Had he been talking to Siobhan on the way home? Wonderful, I could just hear them now. Have you seen Kell, doesn't she look like shit today? Why did I need enemies when I had these two as friends? My scowl deepened.

Mid scooted off my desk and plopped down in his chair, sliding it until it was now across from me, my desk in between us. This was a natural pose we assumed while at work, usually to go over stories or talk about something. It probably looked like we were going to play cards. Actually, we did that too, when things were slow. Given my current aura of animosity and that last brave comment he made, maybe Mid was keeping my desk in between us as protection.

"Your face is pale, your hair looks like a rat's nest and your eyes are all funny looking, kinda glazed over. Have you eaten today? Maybe you just need some food," Mid continued.

By this time I was scowling so hard I thought my eyes would cross. I massaged at the spot between my eyebrows, willing away the line I knew was forming. Really, with two friends like these I'd have a furrow there before I was 30. And food? Why did they both think food was the answer all the time?

"I'm not hungry, Mid. Do you even know what's going on around here? Do you realize the day I've been having?" My voice escalated with each word. "I found a dead girl on the beach this morning, for crying out loud." Across from me, Holly peered around Mid and raised her arched brows even higher.

"Quit looking at me," I snapped.

"Middleton, dear, can you attempt to control her outbursts? Some of us are trying to work, you know. Really, I rather preferred her asleep," Holly purred, deftly tossing her curls over one shoulder.

I shot to my feet, ready to verbally snap her in two. Mid

stood up a half second after I did, ready to grab me if necessary. He put his hands on my shoulders.

"Steady, Rambo. Ignore the lovely Miss Holly. Get your stuff, let's get out of here." Mid draped an arm around me and pulled me along with him as I grabbed my bag. "Don't work too hard, darlin'." He winked at Holly as we shuffled off. She beamed, looking for all the world like the cat who'd eaten the cream.

"Oh, Middleton, remember you're coming with me tomorrow evening for the opening of the new restaurant on East Bay," Holly intoned in her best Southern drawl. I swear she does that just to irritate me, laying on the accent thick as syrup. She knows I wish I'd been born and raised here.

"Right. I'll pick you up at seven," Mid said. Holly fluttered a fingertip good-bye to him.

Oh, how cozy, I thought. She's been trying to get her claws in my unsuspecting pal for a while now, and apparently was succeeding. He was supposed to be dodging her, not escorting her out on the town. My mood wasn't any better as we passed Myra on the way out.

She took her glasses off and let them hang from the colorful beaded chain around her neck. It was the only exception to color in her entire wardrobe, from what I had been able to gather over the years. Black, white, brown and various shades of each were her fashion statements.

"Take care of her, Middleton, she has had a rather rough day," Myra said.

"So I've heard, Myra. I'll do my best," Mid answered, giving her a quick hug.

Myra retrieved her glasses from around her neck, positioning them back into place and reached for the ringing telephone. "Yes, a rather rough day. But don't worry Kell, tomorrow's another day."

Today had been bad. I shuddered to think what tomorrow might bring.

CHAPTER NINE

The air outside felt fresh and breezy, a pleasant change from the oppressive atmosphere the newsroom had taken on. It was mid-May, the height of the tourist season had yet to arrive, but with Memorial Day weekend fast approaching I knew our days were numbered. I put my shades on, slung my bag over my shoulder and trudged a few steps ahead of Mid.

Used to my sulking episodes, he didn't give in and rush to keep up, so I slowed down until we were side by side. The door to Beau's Barbecue Joint stood open, the deliciously sweet and spicy aromas reminding me I'd missed lunch, as usual. Mid put a hand on my arm and guided me inside before I could protest.

"I know you haven't eaten, so let's have at it," he said.

"Did you eat yet?" I asked.

"Yeah, I grabbed something on my way home," Mid answered.

I walked up to the counter where a spread of barbecue beef, rolls, coleslaw, potato salad, lima beans and rice were waiting. Feeling cranky, I passed it up and stopped in front of the ice cream cooler, where decadent decisions awaited. Mid was somewhere behind me engrossed in a conversation with Hiram Pettigrew, one of the City Council members. Hiram enjoys the prestige of being the eldest member, and at eighty-eight years old is pretty hard of hearing. From the way Mid was practically shouting, I figured Hiram had left his hearing aid at home again.

"What'll it be, pretty lady," asked Beau himself, greeting me with an ear to ear grin. In his fifties, Beau Ashley is well over six feet tall with broad shoulders and an affable manner that makes him one of the most liked people in town. He can also cook up a storm. I had once proposed to him over a drunken game of poker just so I could have a live-in chef of my very own, but his wife Laura had beaten me to the punch some thirty-odd years earlier.

"Hey Beau, what's up," I said.

"Same old same old, except business is pretty good for this time of year, so I'd say things are peachy." His grin faded as he studied my face. "Uh, oh. I kinda figured since you were standing in front of the ice cream that you were feeling funky."

My emotions are forever betraying me by showing up without my encouragement. I'm a terrible liar, get teary eyed with joy when someone strikes it big on Wheel of Fortune and get as huffy as a spoiled child when things weren't going my way. Like now.

I frowned at the ice cream selections and since I couldn't choose between Chocolate Peanut Butter and Mint Chocolate Chip I ordered a double dip, one of each. Beau put two generous scoops on a napkin-wrapped sugar cone and handed it over the counter to me. Behind me, Hiram was hollering about the septic tank versus sewer debate Folly was in the midst of.

"So, Kell, you're much too pretty to be sporting that scowl. What's wrong," Beau asked, wiping his big hands on a towel and tossing it aside.

My brother Aidan says I'm like a book he read yesterday, I'm so transparent. I used to think it was the blood bond between us that made him so perceptive to my feelings, but apparently this applied to all others who paid attention, too.

I licked my ice cream. "Did you hear about the dead girl?" I asked.

Beau blew out a breath and shook his head, and with his full head of shaggy white hair he looked like a sad polar bear. "Sure did, Laura got a call from Bonnie earlier. Such a shame, such a shame." His big chest heaved with a sigh. "Things like this just don't happen here."

I nodded, grabbing a drip of Chocolate Peanut Butter with my tongue. Mid appeared at my side, although I could still hear Hiram talking to who ever would listen. "Hi, Beau. I'm sure you've heard about the surfer from this morning." He raised his eyebrows at me when he noticed my luncheon selection.

"Kell and I were just talking about that exact situation, in fact. You're a crime reporter, right? What do you make of it?" Beau asked.

Mid adjusted his shades atop his head and cleared his throat. "Alex filled me in on all the details on my ride back to town, and it's really got me baffled, to tell you the truth. I run in to all kinds of tragedies in Charleston and some of the other towns, but never at Folly. I don't like it."

"Yeah, Cristina says she knew the girl from the water, not real well, but you know how these kids all get to know each other," Beau replied. Cristina is Beau and Laura's seventeen-year-old daughter and an avid surfer.

Mid squared his shoulders. "Listen, Beau, not to be an alarmist or anything, but keep an eye on her, okay? I don't know if this surfing angle will amount to anything, but I've never heard of anything like it."

Beau's bushy eyebrows drew together and his grin was nowhere in sight. His mighty hands were spread out on the counter and his voice betrayed no emotion when he said, "Anyone mess with my daughter and I'll hog tie them to the nearest tree."

I reached across the counter and gave him a quick hug, dripping a bit of ice cream on his shoulder. "Oh, come on now, smile already. Nothing's going to happen to Cristina."

He regarded me with serious eyes, then rewarded me with a grin. "I'll smile if you will, pretty lady."

"Take care, Beau," was the most I could muster.

"Right back at'cha," he replied.

I turned to leave, then remembered something. "Beau, you're on the Planning and Zoning Committee, so you must know when Preston Brooks can motion again to get his property rezoned," I said.

"Never, as far as I'm concerned. That sorry excuse for a local has been making my life miserable since high school. Glad to vote against his request every chance I get."

I gave Beau a real grin this time, making a mental note to ask about their childhood escapades one day.

Mid and I made it to the door before Hiram noticed me, although I'd be seeing him at the council meeting later on. Don't get me wrong, I love the old fellow, but he will talk your ear off and I wasn't in the mood.

We continued up Center Street towards the beach, passing by the Shag Club, The Folly Beach Barber Shop and the little corner market. The mud pit next to the Coast was currently unoccupied. It usually doesn't see much action until the evening hours. There were several Harley's parked out front of the Coast, and the door was open, letting a little light into the dark bar. Through the smoky haze I recognized several of the regulars lined up at the counter.

"Hold up there, little lady," came a rough voice as we passed.

"Oh, shit," Mid said with a sigh.

I was suddenly engulfed in a giant bear hug, lifted off my feet and swung in a circle. "Where'ya been hidin' at," shouted the beast who held me, whooping and hollering. Luckily, I was set back on solid ground before my ice cream decided to make a reappearance.

My head spun for a second as Cyrus Davis gave me a pat on the back, then bestowed a hearty slap on Mid's, causing him to stumble forward with a curse.

"Damn, man, take the cork out of your ass for once, will ya," Cyrus bellowed. Mid straightened up and regained his dignity, although by his pained expression I knew he was not enjoying himself.

"Cyrus, you've got to stop sneaking up on me," I laughed. He's one of the bouncers at the Coast, bald and always dressed in full Harley Davidson regalia. Think Kojak turned biker.

"Come on in and shoot some pool, Kell." He gave Mid the once over. "You can come, too."

Cyrus is always a lot of fun to hang with, and last time Siobhan and I had made a night of it at the Coast he was very helpful in keeping the other bikers away from us. It's a strange place to go, as practically everyone who is anyone mixes easily. On the weekends, bands take the stage and it gets pretty wild. I've seen uptight attorneys and even the mayor himself partying hardy here.

"Oh, Cyrus, I wish we could," I said while Mid gave me the evil eye. "I still have work to do. Maybe we'll see you this weekend."

"Don't know when you're going to stop doing that. Work," he grunted. "All you ever do is work."

I blew him a kiss as we walked away. Now it was Mid's turn to get grumpy.

"I don't know why you let him manhandle you, I really should call your brother and let him know just what sort of people you consort with," he said, hands in his pockets.

"Oh, for heaven's sake, I don't consort with anybody, Cyrus is harmless. It's you who should be ashamed of who you're planning on consorting with."

Mid stopped in his tracks. "Now what in the hell are you talking about?"

"Little Miss Southern Belle, that's who," I declared. I kept walking, forcing Mid to follow behind. We reached the parking lot of the Holiday Inn and walked across to the wall separating it from the beach. I leaned on it, watching surfers take off on either side of the pier and fishermen standing on the giant structure with their poles over the side.

Mid stood next to me. "Oh, I see we're back to Holly again. She's not that bad Kell, you guys just don't have much in common."

"Thank God for that," I snapped.

"So you're mad I said I'd go with her to the new restaurant, is that it? Come on, don't be such a brat," Mid said, reverting to his favorite name for me from childhood.

The familiar term brought unexpected tears to my eyes and I wiped them away with the back of my hand, but not before Mid noticed.

"Okay, what gives? This isn't just about Holly," he said. "Tell me."

"It's that stupid t-shirt she wears, you know the one that says GRITS, for girls raised in the south. She just wears it to work to piss me off."

Mid peered at me closer. "Is it like, possibly that time of the month, because you are not making sense."

No, I suppose someone who had been born and raised in one place wouldn't understand, and as both Mid and Holly had roots dug deep in Charleston, they both qualified. The difference was Mid really didn't know what I was talking about, while Holly had found my weak spot a few years ago and liked to drive the stake home now and then.

I reflected back on the conversation Aidan and I initiated with our parents when we were nine and seven respectively. By this age, I'd already lived in Bolivia, Argentina, California, Texas and Costa Rica. Aidan could add El Salvador to his list. At this stage, we found ourselves in Des Moines, Iowa, surrounded by children who had been raised there and by some very tall corn fields. In fact, it seemed their parents and their parents' parents were all from this one place, which was inconceivable to my brother and me. After a lengthy discussion, we approached our parents as a team, sitting across the kitchen table from them. Being the oldest, Aidan was our spokesperson.

"We want to know where we come from," my brother stated.

My mom and dad exchanged glances. She stood up and went to the bookshelf, bringing a large book titled "Anatomy" back to the table. "I knew this day would come eventually," she said, opening the book. "You see, first a man and woman come together and a tiny thing called a sperm joins with an egg....." I had no clue what she was talking about but Aidan jumped up red-faced and slammed the book shut.

"No! We mean where are we from?"

Apparently my dad understood the question and went to the bookshelf, returning with an atlas. "Well," he began, clearing his throat. "See here? This is New York, where I was born. It's where Granny Palevac was born, too. Gramps came from here, Czechoslovakia," he continued, pointing to a spot on the map. Aidan and I leaned in eagerly, soaking up the information about who we were.

"Your mother was born here, in Scotland, which is where Granny and Grandpa Corrigan were born and where we go when we visit them, remember? And you, Aidan, were born here, in El Salvador. Kell, this is you, right here, Bolivia."

My brother and I sat back in our chairs and looked at each other. "So I guess we're from the world," he said. And that was that.

They've actually coined a phrase for us nomadic children who grow up globally. Third Culture Kids, mainly children of diplomats, aid workers, business executives, journalists and military personnel, reared around the globe. Trust me, it was hard to ever fully penetrate the local culture of any place I resided.

I took a few deep breaths, and tried to explain my feeling to Mid. By the time I was finished, he seemed to get it.

"This is my home, where I'm mainly from now for the first time in my life. I don't care where I was born or where I've lived," I exclaimed.

As we made our way back to the newsroom, Mid made a sudden detour into Mr. Joe's Beach Store. He emerged with a bag, thrusting it at me. I opened it, and pulled out a bright orange t-shirt with Carolina girls, best in the world emblazoned across the front. I changed in my car and drove towards home, wearing my brand new shirt and singing along at the top of my lungs to Lynrd Skynrd telling Neil Young southern man doesn't need him around anyhow.

CHAPTER TEN

It was a little before five o'clock when I pulled in the driveway, meaning I had two hours until the council meeting. I let myself in, inhaling the soothing smells of home, which in my case includes the salty sea air, my lavender geraniums blooming rather nicely by the front window and Fred. It was time for a bath, but somehow I felt in my still sort of frazzled state that I needed one more than he did.

Sampson meowed hello, wrapping himself around my legs as I attempted to make it to the bathroom. He kept up the conversation, his voice changing octaves as he told me about his day. I passed by Fred lounging on his bed in the corner and he thumped his tail on the floor in greeting. My cat was trying to crawl up my legs by now, so I hoisted him over one shoulder and dropped my bag on the floor near my bed.

"Stay here, buddy," I told Sampson as I deposited him on the blankets. "It's bath time for me." I didn't have to repeat myself. He knows the word bath. His ears flattened out against his head and he gave me his mean cat glare, completely prepared to fight it out if faced with the tub.

"Not you, silly. Me," I laughed.

I puttered in to the bathroom, turning the overhead light to a dim setting, and ran the water. My muscles ached all around my neck and shoulders, so I poured in a generous helping of Epsom Salts. I discovered this remedy when I was a competitive gymnast during high school, and again when I was a cheerleader in college. When I quit the cheerleading squad and took up track, the same potion succeeded in soothing all aches and pains.

I undressed, letting my clothes fall in a heap on the floor, piled my hair on top of my head, secured it with a barrette and eased in to the welcoming water.

Looking around the bathroom, I felt a sense of serene contentment, coupled with a bit of pride. I'd painted the walls a pale, shimmery blue, had fluffy white towels rolled up in a big wicker basket on the floor, and hung real sand dollars around the top of the walls as a border. The tile floor is an incredible shade of blue verging on purple, and I'd topped it off with the biggest, most luxurious white bath mat I could find. All in all, my private sanctuary.

I sank down as far as I could, resting my head on the neck pillow and let my thoughts drift. The emotionally charge morning had brought old childhood insecurities of my gypsy upbringing to the surface, probably because I let Holly irritate me so much. I splashed the water a bit, stirring up the Epson Salts. The irony of Holly working at the same place I did was not lost on me.

As freshmen, we both made the cheerleading squad at the College of Charleston. Ask me now why I tried out and I really couldn't say. Tired of gymnastics, it was a natural alternative, and I guess I thought it would be a good way to make friends at my new school. Moving so much had at least given me the resources to make friends fairly easily, and cheerleading sounded exciting.

Having attended the prestigious all girls' school in Charleston, Ashley Hall, Holly was obviously not a newcomer to town, and neither, did it turn out, was the rest of the freshmen squad. As I begun to explore the area, I quickly fell in love with the history and mystery of Charleston. Then I discovered Folly Beach. If Charleston is the grand dame of society, Folly is its wild child.

During the first few weeks of practice, I gushed to the other girls on the squad about the magic and adventure of the Low Country, although for the most part they were a bit jaded regarding my enthusiasm. When the news broke that our star quarterback, a true blue Charlestonian by the name of Charles Heyward, was quite taken with me, all hell broke loose among the previously docile southern ladies of the squad.

I closed my eyes, remembering the look of fury on Holly's face when she confronted me, accusing me of stealing her boyfriend. Completely clueless as to what she was talking about, I had tried to walk away and was surrounded by the other girls. Holly, her hair pulled back in a ponytail so tight it made her eyes stretch, embarked upon a screaming episode detailing the dubious source of my pedigree. I told her to take her prissy attitude and shove it, and she came at me with claws drawn. Now remember, I grew up with a big brother. No cat fight for me. I simply slugged her, dropped my pompoms and quit the squad.

My bath was cooling some, so I ran a little more hot water, opening my eyes. Nine years later Holly could get my goat on occasion although we had long since made our peace with each other, however fictitious. I sighed, stretched in the tub and relaxed for a bit longer.

The tap tap tap of claws on the floor alerted me to Fred's approach. He poked his head in the doorway, saw me reclined in luxury and ambled over to the tub. I sat up, ready just in case. He has the horrible habit of trying to climb in and it makes a complete mess of the place, not to mention the fact that it shocks me so much when I'm not prepared that I practically drown.

He rested his head on the edge and I scratched him behind the ears. When one paw came up beside his head, I figured my bath was over. I pulled the plug, dried off and walked to my closet. Clothes. What to wear. I rifled through the selection, coming up with a pair of decent jeans and a green fitted t-shirt that flattered my eyes. I dressed, tucking the shirt in and topping the outfit off with a well worn leather belt. I am not a clotheshorse. I detest shopping, and most likely only have a wardrobe because my mother shops for me, mailing me various items during the year.

Back in the bathroom I moisturized, combed, dried, curled and painted until I looked presentable enough to face City Council. The clock in the kitchen told me it was almost time to leave, so I opened the fridge, grabbed a slice of cold pizza and a glass of milk. Eating and drinking I walked around, turning off lights and fluffing the pillows on my bed. I was so tired I could have climbed in right then, but I'd never missed a meeting in my life, and one dead body wasn't going to change things.

I left the light on in the living room, grabbed my bag and keys, and flipped the porch light on too. As I was locking my front door, I saw it. A white envelope with my name on it, spelled out in letters cut out and glued on, taped to the door. I glanced around the growing darkness of evening, opened the envelope and pulled out the sheet of paper folded in thirds. Cut out of the same jumbled letters from some magazine or the like was a note. 'HOW DO YOU LIKE HER KELL? I WILL GIVE YOU MORE'.

I shoved it all in my bag and ran to my car.

CHAPTER ELEVEN

I was careening down Ashley Avenue at a rate of speed that would make NASCAR drivers proud. It was dark out, too dark, and I watched as a cloud reached out and grappled with the moon for possession of the night, winning the battle and taking away what little illumination there had been. My fingernails dug into the steering wheel and I couldn't seem to catch my breath. Every so often I glanced over at my bag on the passenger's seat, thinking the thing inside would jump out and get me.

I swerved to miss a raccoon crossing the road, almost plowing into one of the giant rocks at the washout. In my rearview mirror I saw the headlights of a vehicle pull out of its hiding spot on Weather's Lane and begin to follow me. I floored it, and would have probably driven like Mario Andretti all the way to City Hall if the spinning lights on the car behind me along with the siren hadn't brought me to my senses.

Slowing down, I eased over to the side of the road, ready to bolt again if I didn't recognize my captor. Dan Jacoby unfolded himself from his patrol car, pointed a flashlight in my direction and walked up to my window. I was so relieved to see him I slumped forward over my steering wheel for a moment, trying to breathe like a normal person.

"Kell, uh, Ms. Palevac? Are you all right? Can you roll down the window?" Officer Jacoby asked. I straightened up in my seat and complied.

"I'm sorry to pull you over, ma'am, but you were going

55 mile per hour and you almost took out a boulder," he said, blushing furiously.

"Can you get in my car a minute," I gasped.

Jacoby looked side to side, his eyes puzzled and his face practically on fire. "Um, I don't really think I should do that."

I let out an exasperated sigh then held my breath so I wouldn't hyperventilate. The poor boy thought I was trying to seduce him to escape a ticket. "Look, Dan, this is serious. Someone left a letter on my door. If you get in now I'll pretend I didn't hear you call me ma'am."

Officer Jacoby was not responding in the way I intended. Instead, he held his flashlight up higher and blinded me like a deer caught in headlights.

"Ms., um, Palevac? Are you sure you're all right? Have you, um, been, you know, drinking," he asked me.

Instead of hitting my forehead against the steering wheel in frustration, I gently placed it there, which at least spared my eyes from his flashlight. "Dan. Officer Jacoby," I began, speaking to the wheel. "A threatening letter concerning the dead girl was left on my door, I'm sort of scared, so if you aren't getting in the car can I please leave and bring it to someone a bit more concerned?"

The flashlight was lowered as Jacoby said, "Oh, like a death threat or something? Sheesh, did you touch it? Hold on, let me get some gloves."

Did I touch it? How else would I have read it? This was getting to be just a bit too much for me. He opened the passenger door, pointing at my bag. I pulled it on to my lap and he climbed in, pulling on a pair of thin latex gloves.

I opened my bag and was about to reach for the letter when he stopped me, so I held it towards him and let him retrieve the nasty thing himself. I saw disbelief cross his face as he read, turning the paper over and back again.

"Holy shit, uh, sorry, ma'am, but this is weird," Jacoby said, his flushed face now turning a paler shade of white. "It was on your door?"

"Right. On my door, and cut with the ma'am crap, I thought we agreed to that. Listen, I don't have time for this right now, do you think you could bring it to your uncle for me? Here, take the envelope, too." I thrust my bag back towards him.

"Sure, sure, and listen, I'll make sure to drive by your house extra tonight, okay," he said, removing the envelope.

I looked at my watch. Ten minutes until the meeting started. "Thanks," I said. "I've got to go."

"Um, Kell. Please slow down," Officer Jacoby instructed, his boyish face once again turning crimson.

I pulled off, relieved to have passed the buck, although I knew this was far from over. It was also a relief Jacoby didn't write me a ticket. Judge Brooks' shifty eyes flashed in my head. What kind of idiot would take the time to cut out all those letters and risk being seen taping it to my front door? Linski. It was probably just him and Hans messing with me. It was exactly the type of sophomoric thing the two of them would do. Little nerdy Linski was no match for me. My brain conjured up all sorts of retaliatory action and before I knew it, I'd reached City Hall.

I ran up the steps and went inside, took the hall to the right and rushed in through the big double doors to the meeting room. I did a double take. The place was packed. A whistle from the front of the room alerted me to Siobhan's presence, and I did the excuse me, pardon me thing as I made my way through the crowd. She'd saved me a seat in the front row, and I gratefully sank in to the chair.

"I was wondering where you were, you're usually here early," Siobhan said, fiddling with the camera in her hand. She was uncharacteristically dressed in a simple peach-colored cotton dress that clashed with her flaming hair but still managed to look good on her. She fidgeted in her seat, turning around and scanning the place.

The mayor and council members were not in their seats at the large table in front of me yet, so I did the same. I found myself face to face with a furry creature about three feet tall squatting in the chair behind me. His coat was an olive-greenish shade and his face was black, with tufts of olive here and there. His warm brown eyes regarded me quizzically and the large, down turned mouth beneath his crinkled up nose suddenly broke in to a toothy grin as he extended one hairy hand.

"This is Linus, and he must approve of you as he wants to make your acquaintance," proclaimed the elderly gentleman to Linus' right. He had a bright red rope in one hand that I now could see was attached to a multi-colored collar peeking out beneath Linus' fur.

Siobhan and I looked at each other and I did the polite thing. Extending my hand to the baboon, which had to weigh in at about 50 pounds, I was rewarded with a handshake, and then Linus put his other giant paw on top so my hand was now captured. High-pitched monkey sounds erupted from the animal.

"Oh, my, he is quite taken with you, my dear. Of course, they do know instinctively who does and does not like them," continued the slender fellow with the mop of gray hair. "Now, Linus, give the young lady her hand back."

Yes, Linus, I silently agreed, back with the hand already. Linus was stoking it with one of his paws, then drew his mouth together in a large pucker and kissed the top. He made a sad howling sound as I reclaimed my hand.

Now that I was free, I said, "Hello, Linus, it's good to meet you." Siobhan was standing up in her chair, snapping pictures of the crowd behind us, and the baboon twisted his head around so he was almost upside down. Huh, just a second ago I was the object of his affection and now he was trying to get a look up my friend's dress.

"Act like a gentleman, Linus," admonished his owner, pulling on the red rope.

"Would you look at all the animals in here, and I don't mean the regular human ones we usually see," Siobhan shouted to me over the din of voices, snorts, howls and growls. I did the ladylike thing and stood up on my chair for a better view. At least I was wearing jeans.

The place was, quite literally, a zoo. Dotted here and there amongst the sometimes- dubious looking inhabitants of our island were some I definitely didn't recognize. A huge, black pot bellied pig took up most of one of the rows, existing peacefully next to what appeared to be a small brown bear. To my left a few rows back a snake as thick as my arm was draped around Scary Harry's neck. Eye patch in place, Scary Harry looked like he may have bathed for the occasion, and he sported a well-worn gray t-shirt with 'Question Reality' across the front. He waved at me and his snake hissed at me, so I figured I was one for one. I spotted Bonnie McLeod, orange megaphone in hand, shouting orders to anyone who would pay attention. "Hi, Kell," she hollered when she saw me. "Hi, Kell," the room echoed in unison, our merry little band all geared up and ready for some fun. I wiggled my fingers and sat back down in my seat. I'd never seen a council meeting this well attended.

At that moment the side door opened and Mayor George McLeod and the six council members filed in, the mayor squirting his mouth with his ever-present breath spray. A couple of the others were popping breath mints. It's no secret they get together for a mint julep or two before the meetings. From the way things were starting to heat up in here I wished I'd had one myself.

They filed in behind the table and took their seats, three on either side of Mayor McLeod. Joan Darby, a marine biologist and Sandra Crews, real estate agent extraordinaire, are the only female members of council. Hiram Pettigrew sat to the right of the mayor, and next to him was Big Legare, weighing in at nearly 300 pounds. He's an ex-pro wrestler. William Tradd, who claims to be a direct descendant of the first landholder in South Carolina, and Earl Jenkins, who can't even claim to hold a job, round out the group.

Siobhan, who was probably having the time of her life with all the photo opportunities, didn't notice their arrival.

"Quiet down, please, quiet down," Mayor McLeod bellowed through the microphone. "And Ms. Mulvaney, would you please sit down?"

Siobhan turned in her chair and took a quick snap of the seven in front of us before complying. The noisy tones of the people in the room continued, and somewhere towards the back a goat bleated.

Mayor McLeod gestured towards the gavel in front of Hiram, who picked it up and began banging it repetitively as the mayor called the meeting to order. The pack was as close as it was going to get to dead silence, but Hiram kept up with the banging, squinting at us through his thick glasses.

"He forgot his hearing aid again," Siobhan whispered to me and I nodded.

Big Legare caught Hiram's hand just before it cracked the gavel one more time. "They're quiet, Hiram," Big said.

"What?" hollered Hiram.

"They're quiet," Big shouted.

"Well, you don't have to shout, I'm sitting right next to you," muttered Hiram.

Mayor McLeod announced, "The main item on the agenda for this evening's meeting is the Exotic Animal Ordinance, proposed by Bonnie McLeod." Boos and growls rose to a feverish pitch, and Hiram started the gavel thing again. This went on for a few frenzied moments before Bonnie, all five feet of her, stood up on her chair and raised the megaphone to her mouth.

"Cut the crap, and George, whoever said all these animals were allowed here tonight?" she shouted at the room and her husband.

The question produced perplexed looks on the faces of the mayor and council. They turned to one another questioningly, shoulders shrugging and several not me's coming through loud and clear. The noise in the room was once again rising. Linus was on his chair behind me, pounding his chest and making baboon sounds. Apparently several of his kin were also in attendance, their monkey shrieks bouncing off the walls.

"Come on, let's circulate," Siobhan shouted, grabbing my arm. Hiram had the gavel going again and the mayor was standing, calling for order, as we made our way down an aisle, doing our reporter/photographer gig. I quickly scribbled as I recognized the menagerie at hand. Pig, goat, small brown bear, lots of monkeys, something tall and furry, a skunk. I stopped short.

"Don't worry, dear, he's had his scent gland removed,"

shouted Erma, who owns the liquor store. The skunk turned his back on me and raised its tail and I moved as fast as possible towards the back of the room.

"Look, Kell, he's an emu." Siobhan grinned with delight as she snapped pictures of a long-legged creature roughly six feet tall.

"Yep, very fast runners, emus are. This is Ellie," said Ellie's owner, a short, squat fellow with a bandana tied around his head. Ellie proceeded to root around in my hair with her nose, and just as I was really starting to enjoy myself I turned around, laughing, and bumped into Judge Brooks.

He was leaning against the back wall, arms folded across his chest and a scowl on his face.

"Uh, sorry," I said.

His eyes slid up and down me. As if he didn't hear a word, he turned and continued staring straight ahead.

This little exchange was not lost on Siobhan. "My, my, Judge Brooks, I believe the lady apologized to you. Where ever are your manners?"

"Hush, Siobhan," I mumbled.

The shouts, snorts, bellows, squeals and hisses grew louder as Preston Brooks turned his scowl first on Siobhan, then back at me. Bonnie McLeod was up on her chair, hollering who knows what through her megaphone. Just as a chant of "Hell no, we won't go" began rising above the crazed rumbling, Preston Brooks calmly removed a black gun from the holster under his arm. I screamed, grabbing Siobhan and pulling her to the ground with me as he pointed it at the ceiling and fired off a single shot.

A stunned silence followed, with an occasional bleat or snort here and there. All eyes were turned towards Judge

Brooks as he said, "I believe the mayor is calling this meeting to order." He tucked his gun back in the holster. Little pieces of plaster fell from the ceiling and dusted my hair as Siobhan and I stayed down, hands covering our heads.

CHAPTER TWELVE

I awoke the following morning once again to the offensive alarm. Instead of jumping right out of bed, I stayed put for a few minutes, remembering the events of yesterday.

Our city council meetings are rarely boring, but this one had been amazing. After Judge Brooks' assault on the ceiling, several deputies had swarmed the place. Needless to say, the meeting was cancelled. Siobhan quickly recovered her composure and snapped several shots of unruly townsfolk and disgruntled beasts being herded out the doors. We went straight to the newsroom, where I wrote a detailed account of the night's events and Siobhan developed her film. Alex might use the story on the front page if we were lucky.

I lay back with my hands folded behind my head. The sound of the ocean could easily lull me back to sleep if I wasn't careful. Sampson plopped himself down on my belly, doing the little pushy things with his front claws. I felt like a pin cushion. So much for drifting back off.

Chief Stoney had reached me at the paper while I was writing my article, nearly biting my head off for touching the envelope on my front door. Fingerprints and all that. I snapped right back about being a reporter, not an officer of the law, and we continued badgering each other a bit until he apologized and I was properly mollified. Now enlightened as to how one deals with potential evidence, the chief and I said our good-byes to each other, although I did stick my tongue out at the phone after I hung up. I'm sure he did something equally mature on his end.

Sampson was beginning to draw blood. "Off of me," I commanded. He didn't listen. Sitting up, I pushed him gently aside to the tune of his annoyed meow and went in search of coffee. Not one to waste time, I plopped down on the cream-colored ceramic tile floor and stretched my hamstrings. All those years in gymnastics had left me with some pretty great legs, but they tend to cramp up easily if I don't take time to stretch, which I usually don't.

I stood up, leaned against the counter and did a quadriceps stretch. Alternating hands, I gently pulled on each leg. Ouch. No running today. My legs were too tired. The coffee machine made its final last brewing noises and I made my cup and grabbed a banana. Suitably fortified, I walked outside onto my back porch and sat down to assess the morning's arrival.

I love my little back porch. It's almost an enclosure, with the deck upstairs providing shelter and the six-foot fence plenty of privacy. I've adorned the fence with plant holders containing a variety of trailing petunias and baby's breath, and had several terra-cotta pots scattered around which were currently bursting at the seams with a collection of coleus, impatiens and geraniums. I have a very green thumb. Can't cook to save my life, but I sure can garden with the best of them.

I couldn't get the image of Jennifer Donnelly out of my mind. It had been easier yesterday, probably because I was in a state of semi-shock. Now, as I smelled the salt air and sipped my deliciously creamy coffee, trying to think about my upcoming day, her face kept intruding. Eyes open and unseeing. Beautiful golden hair floating in the ocean. Ugly red marks around her neck.

"Get out of my head," I commanded her, but she wouldn't. This was not going to do. I could not start my day like this. I jumped to my feet.

"Sorry, Jenny, can't sit around and obsess about you. Not a healthy way to start the day," I said.

"Who are you talking to, Kell," a voice asked from above. For a second I thought it was someone from really up above, until I looked up and saw a single brown eye peering down through the boards of the deck.

I let out an exasperated sigh. "Elbie, what are you doing? Are you spying on me again? I thought your mother told you not to do that anymore."

The eye stayed put. "I wasn't spying on you Kell, really. I just woke up. I heard voices," Elbie said.

Uh huh. I bet you hear voices all right, I thought.

"Who are you talking to, anyways," he tried again.

"Nobody. Just myself."

"My mom says I shouldn't do that. Talk to myself. She says it's strange. And will make people wonder. What exactly do you think they'll wonder, Kell?"

What to say, what to say. I was getting a kink in my neck from looking up at the eye. "Yikes, Elbie, look at the time. I gotta get going. Think I'll take a bike ride before work," I said, heading for my back door.

"Wait, can I come? Please? I love bike riding." The eye was gone, most likely heading for its own back door.

"No, Elbie," I shouted. "You have to get ready for school! Maybe another time."

"No fair," he muttered. "Nobody's ever fair to me. I don't like school anyways."

His voice trailed off as I scooted inside. Something had to be done to get my day going, and a bike ride actually sounded pretty good. I did the whole bathroom routine, pulled on shorts and a tank top and grabbed my cell phone and mace. When I bike, I always head to the east end of the beach, all the way to the end. It's pretty deserted there, and even with Fred along for company I felt better with some protection. Sure, Fred looks frightening, but looks are deceiving.

Right now said Fred was snoozing on his doggy bed, which resembles a small mattress covered in a cute little pattern of doggy bones. I try to let him sleep in as late as possible, but enough was enough. "Up, buddy," I coaxed. "Time to rise and shine."

Fred's right ear twitched as if to shoo away a fly. He heard me, he was just ignoring me. I knelt down and pushed on him, heard Sampson's irritated growl and realized the cat was curled up on Fred's other side. "Fred, get up. Come on! Up!"

He yawned and slowly rose to his feet, standing a bit unsteadily and tried to focus. He looked down where Sampson was happily sleeping the morning away and decided to join him once again. I grabbed my shrieking cat out of the way right before Fred plopped down on top of him.

A trick, something to wake the sleeping giant. I went back to the kitchen and opened the refrigerator. Well, this was interesting. Food. I couldn't remember when I went grocery shopping. Usually I call Mazo's Market for deliveries at the last minute, which means right before I starved to death. There were, however, a few choices with which to entice he who sleeps too much. Milk. I checked the date, opened it, and grimaced. Down the sink it went. A round of brie, too good for Fred. Something that looked like leftover spaghetti with strange fuzz growing on it. A package of lunch meat. I opened it, sniffed, and decided the smoked turkey would do.

Fred was snoring. I held my offering under his snout. It twitched, and he opened his mouth but not his eyes.

"No way, buster. You can forget it. You aren't eating this without waking up," I said and backed away a few steps.

Apparently, he knew the game was up. He stretched. I backed up a couple more steps. He opened his eyes, observing from afar. I dangled the slice of meat. He sneered, but he did arise. I had the leash ready and snagged him at the same time he swallowed the morsel in a fast gulp. Only thing Fred does fast is eat.

My bike is a shiny yellow beach cruiser, complete with a shiny metal basket on front for storing the multitude of treasures the sea so kindly deposits on the sand. I love beachcombing. I stuck my cell and my mace in the basket and Fred stuck his head in, too.

"Nope, you're too big. Really, Fred, you need the exercise." And with that we were off, crossing the road and walking over the dunes. Well, I was off and Fred lagged behind like a pig being led to slaughter.

The tide was low enough that riding on the beach would be relaxing, with plenty of hard-packed sand available. I hopped on my bike and held Fred's leash. We meandered along. I wanted to go faster and Fred didn't want to go at all. We settled for a happy medium.

The sky was a whirl of wispy clouds with streaks of sunlight all fighting for center stage, shimmering off the ocean and bathing the morning in a pinkish hue. I looked heavenward and said a prayer of thanks for being alive and living here and for my mom, dad, brother, friends. Fred and Sampson. My eyes began to tear up and I wished for my shades but I left them behind. My tires crunched over the piles of tiny shells along the water's edge, and I dropped Fred's leash, pumping my legs harder and flying faster and faster.

Winded, I paused and looked over my shoulder. Fred was trotting a good ways behind, but trotting nevertheless. He stopped in his tracks and sat while I watched. This is a sign. It means, "I have found a starfish that has fallen and can't get up," or rather, a starfish caught in the sand too far from the outgoing tide to have a chance of surviving the noonday sun. Dutifully, I about faced and rode back to help.

"Good job, fur face, I was going too fast to see him." I patted Fred and picked up the starfish. It was medium size, with lots of tickly feet seeking water. I carried it and delivered it back to its watery home, watching with satisfaction as it sank into the sand and soaked up the relief. I could almost hear it say a grateful thank-you.

"You know, Fred, if I'm ever out of a job we could start a rescue service. Starfish Saviors, that could be us," I said. He woofed in agreement.

Together we made our way to the far, far end of the island, passing the deserted Morris Island lighthouse and avoiding the heavy pluff mud spewing up enough oysters to feed an army. I was heading to what I call Crab Island, which is actually just a section of the shore teaming with shells of many shapes and sizes inhabited by an array of fiddler and hermit crabs. It's like a town of crabs, tucked around the bend of Folly's east end. Some of the shells are so old they're encrusted with barnacles. Some are so bleached out they look like bones.

Rounding the curving corner, I slowed down and jumped off my bike, laying it down in the sand. I sat beside it and watched the slowly moving procession of shells as they promenaded around their town. Fred came and plopped down next to me, put his head on my knee and watched, too. I scratched his head for him, and he rolled over on his back, so I scratched his belly, too. We sat like that for a while, and then I got up to do a closer inspection of the various shells, looking carefully inside to see if one I fancied might be inhabited. I never, ever, take anything living from the beach. Not a sand dollar, starfish or a shell providing shelter for a crab. I was awarded with three beauties today, a whelk, a periwinkle and a tiny tulip shell so old it had hairline fractures.

I tucked them all into the soft muslin bag I keep in my basket, packed my phone and mace around them, and got back on my bike. It was beautiful here, and I felt so much better. Ready to start my day. Ready for anything. Recharge and invigorated, ready for a challenge. That's me, I thought, Kell the reporter, ready to leap tall buildings in a single bound. Well, at least ready to deal with my editor.

"Let's go, fur face." Fred lackadaisically got to his feet, shaking off sand and sniffing the crabs good-bye. I took off, ready to round the corner on my way back to my comfortable abode, ready still. Ready, ready, ready.

I picked up speed, giggling out loud I felt so good. I stood up on my pedals and really went for it, peddling with all my might as I came around the curve. My head was down and I was hoofing it now. Ready, ready, ready.

I never saw her. I crashed head on into something stretched across my path and did a header over the top of my handlebars. My head collided resoundingly with the earth with a satisfying thud and I landed on my back, my bike careening off for parts unknown.

"Ready or not," I murmured as the sky above me faded from pink to white, then to gray, and finally, to black.

CHAPTER THIRTEEN

The sun was annoyingly hot on my face. My eyelids attempted to flutter open, but found the light too painful. My arms and legs felt heavy and my long, thick hair trapped somehow. I squinted, and from my current position could only look upwards. The sky was an amazingly clear blue, with swirls of wispy clouds marching past too fast for my liking. My head spun.

I felt something alive moving on my left leg advancing gently forward towards my chin. Bending my eyes downward as much as I could, I deduced it to be a human creature about six inches tall. He had a bow and arrow in his hands, and a quiver at his back. Ah, yes, I was Jonathan Swift, most recently of the ship the Antelope which had capsized at sea and this was an inhabitant of Lilliput, where I had washed ashore.

"Captain Prichard," I cried. "Where are you? A Lilliputian is after me!" I lifted my head again to view the creature advancing forward. I squinted, trying to get him in focus.

"Who's Captain Prichard, Kell," a voice asked directly behind me. I tilted my head backwards and rolled my eyes in that direction. My hair yanked tighter at my scalp. There was a rather large human sitting cross-legged right behind my head and smack dab on my hair. I felt a heaviness at the other end of my body, and shifted my eyes in that direction. Something resembling a horse was resting across both of my legs, licking my toes. The horse was making plaintive little howling noises.

"What's a putian, anyways? Why's your bike way over there? I found one of your shells and put it on your leg so you'd see it when you woke up," the voice continued. "Fred's squishing your legs, Kell, and he's starting to bug me with his cryin' and all."

I raised my head as far as I could considering the pressure on my hair and slowly the blurred object on my torso was clear. A small shell moving along motored by its horseshoe crab tenant. Huh, guess one wasn't empty. Further down, the horse morphed into my friend Fred.

"Hey, buddy, what's the matter? Stop with the toes, okay?" I smiled as I recognized my dog. He pointed his snout skyward and howled. I glanced backwards again and searched out the owner of the voice. Elbie. Oddly enough, relief flooded through me at the sight of him. Gulliver's Travels is one of my favorite adventures, but I didn't want to bring the story to life.

I struggled to sit up, and was rewarded with a roaring sound in my skull. My head felt like it was splitting in two. Gingerly, I searched with my fingers and felt a lump in the back. My hand came away sticky. Blood. Great. Now what had I gotten myself into?

"Kell, why are you sleeping next to that girl on the surfboard? Should we wake her up, too," Elbie asked.

I jerked my head from side to side, creating a whiplash effect as I was still nicely pinned down by my friend and neighbor. Back to the left I looked. Sure enough, about six feet in that direction was a surfboard resting in the sand with a young-looking blond resting on top. In profile, she appeared to be asleep but something about her stillness was sending off warning sounds in my damaged cranium.

"Will you two get off of me," I shrieked. I reached back and pulled my hair out from under Elbie as he scrambled to his feet. My legs propelled Fred away with a strength I didn't know they possessed, and I scurried crab-like in the opposite direction of the girl.

Panting, I remained crouched low to the ground. So this is what I had gotten myself into. My breath came in shallow gulps and I started to hiccup. Fred slid along on his belly until he reached my side and stuck his head under my armpit.

"What's the matter with you guys? People think I'm weird, well, you two are actin' weirder'en me," Elbie declared with a snicker. He shook his head. "I think you've been out in the sun too long, Kell, it'll make you sun punched, that's what my mom always says." He ambled off towards the girl.

"Sun punched," he continued. "Sounds like the sun just reaches down and wham! Punches you upside the head."

Elbie was standing directly above her now. I hiccupped and Fred mewed into my armpit. My head felt ten sizes too big and the scene swam fuzzily before me. In slow motion I watched as Elbie squatted down and reached out to shake the girl's shoulder.

"No, Elbie, don't touch anything," I hiccupped as loud as I could.

"Hey, you, wake up," he said, jostling the girl. Too late. "Wake up, will ya? Shit, she's frozen solid, Kell." Elbie stood up and stared down at her. A furious reddish blush began at his neck and quickly spread to his cheeks. He backed away.

"She, she's nekkid," he gulped. "I mean, she's got this elasticy purple thing on top but nothin' on the bottom."

He scampered over to where I remained crouched with Fred and flopped down beside me, hiding his head in my other armpit. Soon his hiccups echoed mine. Fred kept howling, and together we huddled there for awhile in three-part harmony.

Keeping my eyes averted from the girl, I spotted my bike wedged in a clump of beach grass a few feet away. Too dizzy to stand up, I crawled on all fours towards it. "Crap, ouch, damn," I sang out as briars attached themselves to my appendages. I felt around in the matted-down area and emerged victoriously with cell phone in hand.

"Crap, ouch, damn." I made my way back to my companions who were both on their stomachs with their heads covered. Why was I always the one in charge? Instinctively, my fingers went to dial Alex, but, hey, was I going to make the same mistake twice? No siree.

"Folly Beach police station," chirped a reply.

"Connie? It's Kell," I hiccupped.

"Who? Quit burping, I can't understand you. Who is this?"

I held my breath and let it out in a whoosh. "It's Kell. I'm hurt." Hiccup.

"Kell Palevac? Okay, honey, where are you?" Connie replied.

I held my breath again and quickly answered, "On the far east end of the beach. All the way at the end."

"Okay, Adams and Bresseau are out patrolling the water in the john boat, I'll send them your way. Jacoby's testing out the new beach patrol cruiser, so I'll send him, too," Connie said.

"Thanks," I said. "And Connie? Ask them to hurry."

CHAPTER FOURTEEN

I heard the approaching drone of an engine within minutes and struggled to my feet, shaking off my comrades amidst their anguished howls of dismay. Really, they couldn't hide in my armpits indefinitely, and as I was the oldest and therefore the most responsible, I simply had to stand up. Immediately, the girl on the surfboard was in my direct line of vision. I hiccupped and felt like I was going to puke. Okay, so I'd stand up, but that was it. I was not going to look at her.

Officers Clyde Bresseau and Ted Adams appeared in the police department's 16-foot john boat, with Adams at the wheel. He skillfully pulled up close to the shoreline, dropped anchor, and jumped overboard into the shallow water.

"Kell, what's wrong," Adams shouted in my direction. "Bresseau, bring the first aid kit!"

I smiled weakly and gave him a little flutter of fingers as acknowledgment. The sky spun ominously and black spots swam before my eyes. I squatted down and was quickly engulfed by one large dog and one large boy. We nestled together, a hiccup here, a howl there.

Bresseau splashed over the side of the boat, all five feet six of him, first aid kit held high above his head. The water was up to his waist and he bravely waded through, clutching the box tightly.

"Got it, Adams, I'm coming," he huffed loudly, splashing and breathing hard.

Our rescuers rallied towards the shore swiftly and unscathed, all systems go, ready to save the damsel in distress. They marched in our direction and pulled up short. Adams plowed in to Bresseau, who promptly dropped the first aid kit in the sand.

"What in the heck?" Adams exclaimed.

"Who the hell is she," Bresseau asked indignantly. The two officers held their ground admirably, mouths gaping and eyes fixated on the sight of my most recent discovery. Bresseau repositioned himself so he was behind Adams, who still hadn't moved a muscle. A solid, barrel-chested six-footer with a military style flat top, Adams was my choice to hide behind, too, except I couldn't seem to muster the energy to get up.

Elbie emerged from his catatonic state and jumped to his feet, using his hands as blinders on either side of his face as he beelined it towards the men.

"Can't look, can't look," he sing-sang. "Don't look, don't look, don't look. Nekkid girl, no clothes on, can't look." He came to a halt in front of the still motionless officers, whose view was now blocked by the overgrown teenager.

Adams stared at Elbie. He peered around him. "Is he yours, Kell," he inquired incredulously.

"Nope, not mine," I scratched Fred's ear. "He's mine." Fred moaned.

Bresseau stepped out from behind Adams and faced Elbie, who was still ranting on about the unfortunate naked girl on the board. "Can't look, don't look, never, ever look."

"Listen, buster," Bresseau said, craning his neck back so he could look up at Elbie. He adjusted his horn-rimmed glasses. "Cut it out, and get out of the way."

"No, no, no, don't look!" Elbie still had his hands up to his head, and even though I'm pretty used to his oddness I was beginning to get a little worried.

"Elbie, come back over here and sit down with us," I tired weakly, my voice hoarse.

Adams was assessing the situation discreetly, but Bresseau came on like gangbusters. Why is it always the little guys who have to be tough?

"Okay you head case, get out of the way," Bresseau put his hands on Elbie's shoulders and struggled to budge him.

My neighbor was quickly on a lunatic flight toward destruction. He threw his arms up, fists balled, and banged poor Bresseau upside the head. Adams turned with a quick snap of his thick shoulders and tackled Elbie at the same time Bresseau went down.

I breathed an exasperated sigh and gave a helpless wave of my hand. "Over here, remember? Come on, guys, ease up." Oh, forget it, I thought, leaning back on Fred. I'll just lie back down and go to sleep.

I closed my eyes, listening as Elbie shrieked as someone snapped a pair of handcuffs on him. Bresseau was hollering things not becoming to an officer on duty. They were all beginning to fade away quite nicely when the scrunch of bicycle tires echoed in my ears.

"Kell? Kell, wake up, sit up, let me see what's wrong with you," intruded as I was drifting back off to Lilliput. I looked up in to Jacoby's face, his brow knitted with worry. Funny, I'd never noticed his eyes before. They were a heavenly shade of blue, flecked with gray and green.

"You have the most beautiful eyes," I murmured. Jacoby flushed. He reached behind my head and came up with the same interesting blood I'd discovered earlier.

"And you have a giant bump on your head and probably have a concussion," he said. "Sit up, you can't go to sleep." He propped me up against Fred, which allowed me a front row seat to the unfolding drama.

Elbie was lying face down in the sand, hands cuffed behind his back with Bresseau parked right on top of him. Adams had made it over to the girl and Jacoby hurried off in that direction. Through the roaring din in my head I could barely make out what they were saying.

"Dead......frozen solid.....same rope as........", said Adams. "......marks on her hands?......Kell again, strange........" said Jacoby. "Call it in.........hospital."

Odd, I thought as I slid down Fred's side on my way to la-la land, that they'd be taking a dead girl to the hospital. Funny, too, how none of this seemed real. Must be a joke. Okay, I can take a joke, just need to rest a bit. The sun, which was earlier such a severe nuisance, now warmed me, and I soaked up the healing rays as oblivion took over.

CHAPTER FIFTEEN

I spent the better part of the day in downtown Charleston at St. Francis Xavier Hospital, a perfectly good hospital as far as hospitals go, but I have a sincere phobia of the places. I'd seen the inside of far too many emergency rooms in my wild and willful youth, the result of having been egged on by an older brother. When Siobhan and Mid showed up to escort me home, I was ready, willing and able.

"Here are your discharge papers," intoned the emergency room doctor. "You have a mild concussion, nothing serious showed up on the MRI, but try to take it easy for at least twenty-four hours." She flipped through the chart in her hands, making notes.

I took in my stark surroundings, noting the dismal gray walls and starched white sheets I rested on. Everything was shiny silver metal and smelled like ammonia mixed with disinfectant. Emergency room décor hadn't changed much over the years.

I glanced at the doctor's nametag. "Dr. Foresberg, ever hear of a rare condition where someone just starts finding dead bodies in their path?"

A flash of bemusement crossed the doctor's face and she cleared her throat, eyeing me warily. Before she could answer, Siobhan materialized in the doorway.

"What a joker she is, isn't she doctor? Why, just last year she had me searching for leprechauns at the end of rainbows, how'd you like that," Siobhan rambled, waving the cowboy hat she held in her hands. "And then there was the time we borrowed my sister's baby and placed him in the woods, waiting to see if fairies would come to whisk him away."

"Ladies, ladies, I do believe it's time to depart," said Middleton, stepping in to the little room. His hair was tousled from probably having the top down in the Mustang and he ran his fingers through it. Besides the hair thing, Mid looked like the well-bread Charlestonian he is, right down to his neatly pressed, faded jeans. Yep, Mid irons his jeans. I practically fainted when I made that discovery. I guess one could deduce Mama Calhoun raised him well, but it always struck me as a bit overboard. On the other hand, he comes in handy when I need something ironed. He's a pro.

"Thank-you, Dr. Forsberg, I'll be sure to get Ms. Palevac home safely." He removed the papers from the doctor's still outstretched hand and smiled warmly at her, his eyes crinkling up around the edges.

Dr. Forsberg returned his smile, flustered. She smoothed down her graying hair and fussed with her stethoscope. "Oh, Mr. Calhoun, I didn't realize you were here. How are your parents?"

Siobhan and I looked at each other and rolled our eyes. Mid has this effect on women, young and old alike. We attribute it to his smooth good looks, but in this case I think it had something to do with his parents' sizeable contributions to the hospital.

"Just fine, just fine, Dr. Forsberg, thanks for asking. Are you able to attend the charity event my mother is hosting at the house this weekend," Mid asked, giving me the once over and touching the bandage at the back of my head questioningly. I shrugged my shoulders at him.

"Oh, my, yes, I wouldn't miss it for the world. Please say hello for me," Dr. Forsberg said, smile brightening. She turned and left the room, glancing back curiously at Siobhan and me.

I should point out that when Mid casually mentions "the house", he's referring to his parents' 18th century mansion on the Battery in downtown Charleston. It's a daunting expanse with a security system that has everything but a moat filled with alligators. I should know, I used to set all the alarms off at the place before I learned how to properly announce myself.

The three of us walked down the hall towards the exit doors. At the nurses' station, three young ladies stopped chatting and stared at us, or Mid rather, who nodded at them as they blushed. Same nurses who earlier wouldn't give me the time of day when I kept asking how long the doctor would be.

"Bye, I'm fine, thanks," I waved to them as they batted their eyelashes in unison at Mid's retreating figure. "Don't bother to see me out."

Siobhan put an arm around my shoulder. "Don't worry, girl, I love ya. He does kind of make you feel invisible sometimes, doesn't he now?"

"It's a wonder how we exist," I agreed.

The wind was suddenly sweet, the air pungent as we crossed the Ashley River by way of the James Island connector. A smudge of sun still dappled through the cloud cover as the evening approached. I was in the back seat of Mid's convertible, top down, and I let the breeze blow through my bruised head, a natural balm to the offenses of the day. I watched the gigantic American flag billowing from its shaft atop the restaurant below, and listened intently as Mid talked on his cell phone.

"Yeah, she's okay, we're bringing her home. Alex, don't you think this could wait until tomorrow? Well, no, they didn't want to keep her overnight, but, still........, okay, yeah, sure, bye."

Siobhan leaned over in the passenger seat and whispered something to Mid. He faced forward, intent on the road, and answered. I hate sitting in the back.

"What are you guys talking about? What did Alex want," I shouted above the noise of the rushing wind.

Siobhan turned around in her seat, holding on to her cowboy hat with one hand. Her hair whipped around her head with the ferocity of a hurricane. I could see her concern for me reflected in the deep green pools of her eyes, and I was touched.

"Darlin', Chief Stoney wants to come by to visit in a little while, nothing difficult, just a few questions about your exciting morning," she said. "Mid and I will be right there with you, so don't worry."

I am a fiercely independent creature and despised being mollycoddled, having my hand held or anybody's sympathy. I sighed. My head hurt. I had discovered another apparently dead body. I seriously wanted my mom. Under the circumstances, these two would do just fine.

"Okay," I sighed again. Siobhan raised her eyebrows and gave me a sidelong look. Me defeated was not the norm.

The connector deposited us uneventfully onto James Island and we spent a quiet few minutes until we reached Folly. The ride from Center Street took forever, as Mid strictly adheres to the 30 miles per hour speed limit. Me, I can make it a whole lot quicker.

By the light of the setting sun I could just make out the shape of the black, elongated vehicle parked in one of

Ludmilla's spots outside our house. I slumped lower in my seat and smacked my forehead with my open palm. Ouch. Not a good idea. A 1970 Cadillac, low to the ground and menacing. The Batmobile. Why did Murphy have to show up now?

"Quick, Mid, park and let's get inside," I said, scrambling over Siobhan on my way out of the car.

"For the love of God, Kell, get off of me," Siobhan huffed as I scurried away. I was at my front door before the car turned off.

I turned the key and motioned for them to hurry it up. Normally, I can handle Murphy. Elbie and Chief Stoney thrown in to the mix, no thanks. My day had been wrought with enough danger.

I switched on the lights, made for my bedroom, and was greeted by the sight of my beloved animals curled up together on my bed. Fred knows better. He must be taking the morning extra hard. I sat down and scratched a chin here and an ear there.

"Kell, girl, where's the wine opener at? I swear, I don't see how you find anything in these drawers, everything's all jumbled together," Siobhan hollered from the kitchen.

"It's there, just keep looking," I shouted back. I gave my fuzzy family a few last tickles and closed my door. I undressed, letting the tank top and shorts I had thrown on a lifetime ago fall to the floor.

I let the shower steam up the entire bathroom before I got in. The heat melted away the tension in my knotted-up neck muscles, and I took deep breaths of the vaporized water. I closed my eyes, reveling in the luxury. Jennifer Donnelly's face appeared, superimposing itself on to that of the new dead girl. I hadn't gotten a good look at her on purpose, but my mind was making up for that, thank-you very much. Now the two were merging as one. How was I ever going to keep my dead girls straight at this rate?

"No," I groaned, sinking to the floor of the tub. What in the world was going on? I grabbed the shampoo and mechanically washed my hair, added conditioner and sat there for the required three minutes. Tangles gone, I rinsed. Maybe I could just hibernate in here for a few days, grow gills and stay submerged in the tub.

There was a knock at the bathroom door, followed by the sounds of it opening on its squeaky hinges. Privacy is not on the menu when Siobhan comes over.

"You still in there, Kell? Here I brought you a glass of merlot. Came straight from Mid's collection so it's probably grand," she said. The shower curtain was pulled back. If Siobhan thought it was unusual to find me sitting in the tub with the shower raining down upon me, she didn't mention it. She just adjusted the shower head so it missed me a bit, handed me my glass and closed the curtain again.

"Mid's out in the kitchen cutting up cheese and genoa and he brought crackers, too, so when the chief gets here we'll have something to offer him. Besides, I know you haven't eaten all day," she said. I could hear her rummaging through my make-up drawer, sifting through the various new lotion samples I was hording.

"Don't use my samples," I mumbled from my watery enclosure.

"What did you say?"

"My samples of lotion. Don't go using them." I took a gulp of wine.

"You're going to have to come out of there if you want to talk, I can't understand a blimey word you're saying. Have you tried this one? Kelp So Smooth. It's delicious," Siobhan said.

I took another swallow of merlot and reached forward, turning off the faucets. Just one of the many reasons I like to live alone. Privacy. And nobody messing with my stuff. Siobhan and I met on the track team in college shortly after my ill-fated cheerleading career and became fast friends. She comes from a boisterous brood of eight similarly uncontrollable siblings, all red-headed creatures who traipsed and trampled through childhood heedless of the sanctity of belongings. We decided to room together for a while, and her natural tendency to share reached levels beyond my tolerance. Nothing was sacred. My clothes became our clothes, as did any toiletry items. I'd arrive home after a grueling day and find the living room strewn with various people drinking my Coronas and eating my ice cream, which Siobhan would readily replace, but it was just the point. When the point got sharp enough I decided we needed our own space for the sake of our friendship.

I got out of the shower, wrapped up in my oversized purple cotton robe, and watched while Siobhan massaged Kelp So Smooth into her freckles. She had her wavy mane twisted up and secured with one of my copper barrettes, my favorite one, actually, the one with the Celtic knots carved in it.

"What are you mumbling about? Here, try this stuff," she said, pushing my wet hair away from my face and plopping little dollops of lotion on my forehead and cheeks. "Now rub it in."

Dutifully, I complied, examining my face in the mirror next to hers. Siobhan has the face of a fawn, or some other mystical forest creature. We're the same age, but the fine lines around her cat-shaped green eyes have deepened more than mine due to the time she spends squinting through a camera lens. She's fanatical about sunscreen, too, and her skin is pale and dotted with freckles, with a glowing, luminous quality.

She's easily the most charismatic person I've ever met, and I used to have dreams of her as a sister-in-law, but so far my stubborn, bull-headed brother has resisted her charms, and vice versa. I wrinkled my nose in the mirror. Maybe next time Aidan came to visit I'd try my matchmaking again.

My morning escapade at the beach had left my face sunburned across my cheeks and nose. Maybe Kelp So Smooth wasn't such a bad idea, I thought, rubbing it in. My unruly eyebrows were in need of plucking and my hazel eyes were bloodshot, which actually brought out the green in them a bit more, with pale lavender circles underneath. I ran my hands through my hair, my way of combing it out, and practiced a smile. At least my teeth were shiny white and straight, thanks to my mother's diligence in regard to dentists and orthodontists.

"So, are you up for the chief? You haven't even told Mid and me all the details yet," Siobhan said, taking her hair out of the clip and shaking it back. She twisted the lid of my Forever Pink lipstick and applied it expertly, puckering up for the mirror.

I drained my glass of wine and set it next to her empty one on the bathroom counter. This was all happening so fast it was unreal. Yesterday I awoke facing a normal day, then a dead body, and now today, another one. Was I ready to face the chief? Not on your life. Siobhan and I stared at each other in the mirror. She handed me the lipstick, but I shook my head.

"It looks better on you than me, actually," I said.

She rummaged through my drawer, coming up with Honey Gold, and handed it to me. I wasn't in the mood for makeup, so I shook my head again and she shrugged her shoulders, reaching for one of my perfume bottles and spritzing herself.

"Aidan's supposed to be coming to visit soon," I said, crossing my fingers at the white lie and gauging her reaction.

"Well, tell the lad to shower this time, he's always covered in dust from top to bottom," she replied, swishing her hair back. I saw her eyes flare up with interest for one quick second before she recovered herself. Aha! I made a mental note to call my brother and invite him over. If I could find him. Aidan is an archaeologist currently doing biblical research somewhere in the Middle East, but I had his cell phone number or I'd email him. I smiled innocently at my dear friend.

"Ladies, come out, come out wherever you are," Mid rang out, snapping me back to the business at hand. "Company's arrived."

CHAPTER SIXTEEN

By the time I emerged from my room, modestly dressed in a pair of gray sweatpants and an oversized College of Charleston t-shirt, Mid and Siobhan had the festivities in hand. Mid was nursing a Heineken, Siobhan had refilled her wine glass and my old, oak-planked coffee table was adorned with appetizers and two cups of coffee. The table shone in the light from the lemon oil I rub on it regularly, and I knew the carpets were freshly vacuumed and free of fur. My house was ready for visitors even if I wasn't.

I studied the group from afar. Siobhan's singsong lilt was humming on melodiously, no evidence of her spitfire tongue in sight as she chatted with the stranger on my couch. Mid was engrossed in conversation with Chief Stoney, oblivious to my presence. I was exhausted, and the one glass of wine had gone straight to my head. I was just turning to sneak off to my room and let the others carry on when Chief Stoney's booming voice stopped me in my tracks.

"Kell, there you are, come over here and meet Detective Alston," he said.

Drat, I'd been spotted. I drew myself up straight and turned back towards my waiting audience. Walking over, I reached out to shake the hand offered by the stranger.

"Ms. Palevac, good to meet you, I'm Detective Richard Alston with the City of Charleston," he said, standing. We shook, and I assessed the man. He had a masculine presence about him, full of certainty and self-importance. His handshake crushed my fingers. Too much testosterone here, I thought. Siobhan, apparently, was being sucked in to his manly vortex, as she continued to stare with unabashed interest at our new acquaintance. I wrinkled my nose at her.

I sat down in the loveseat next to her and reached for a cracker and cheese. "Hi, everyone."

Chief Stoney cleared his throat and patted his shirt pocket. I raised my eyebrows at him. No way was he smoking in my house. He flushed and dropped his hand, reaching for his cup of coffee.

"Kell, we've brought the Detective on board to try to make some sense of what's going on around here," he said. "You all agree this is highly unusual for Folly."

Mid walked to the kitchen and poured a glass of wine, brought it back and set it on the table in front of me. I reached for it gratefully and took a long swallow.

"Definitely, Chief, we're all in agreement here. One murder was strange enough, but two? And for Kell to find them both? What's up with that," Middleton asked.

"That is exactly what I'd like to ask Ms. Palevac," Detective Alston smiled at me, a suspicious looking smile that didn't reach his eyes.

"Please, call me Kell, and since you're the detective, why don't you answer your own question," I spat, sitting up ramrod straight. The wine was fortifying me and I was starting to feel like myself again. Mid was standing behind me and he reached out a hand and placed it on my shoulder.

Detective Alston adjusted the collar of his Oxford button-down dress shirt and uncrossed his legs. The sooty gray color of his slacks matched the shade of his curling hair and the empty eyes he had trained on me. He leaned forward.

"Ms. Palevac, or Kell, how did you happen to be in precisely the exact spot on two separate occasions where two possibly connected corpses appeared practically out of thin air," he inquired. "Did you know either girl?" He flipped open a small notebook. "Jane Doe number two has been identified as Darla Simmons, by the way."

"You're a detective? You sound more like a horse's ass to me," I shouted, slamming my glass down on the table. "What do you think this is, interrogate Kell time? I don't think so, and if you don't watch it I'll throw you out of my house! I thought you were here to try to solve this mess I'm in. Now you're practically accusing me of being involved somehow."

The chief stood up. "Settle down now, Kell, let the man do his job."

I jumped to my feet, eye to eye with Strom Stoney. "Did you tell him about the letter on my front door? What? Do you think I'm practicing with scissors and leaving myself cryptic notes?"

Siobhan pulled on my arm until I was sitting next to her again, although I couldn't quite catch my breath. Her bemused look belied the indignation I caught reflected in her eyes. "Really, Detective, Kell isn't nearly as dangerous as she looks. More coffee?" she asked, raising the pot.

Detective Alston's jaw muscle worked and he turned bright red. His granite eyes radiated some serious anger as he bore holes through me. As he opened his mouth to reply, his eyes focused on something behind me and changed to round saucers of horror.

Fred had chosen this moment to make his presence known, probably alerted by my raised voice. He ambled over and stood next to me, staring quizzically at the now visibly quaking man before him. I quickly decided not to tell Detective Richard Alston he was in mortal danger of being licked to death.

I placed my hand on Fred's neck. "Steady, boy. Don't be too concerned, Detective, he only attacks upon my command."

"Achoo," he sneezed. "I'm severely allergic to dogs."

Sampson came around the corner of the couch, rubbing his body along its length and scenting all the available feet with the sides of his face. He demurely leapt up on to the detective's lap, circling in the hopes of settling down.

Detective Alston jumped up and unceremoniously dumped my cat to the ground. "I'm allergic to cats, too," he sneezed again. I smiled sweetly.

Mid gave me a behave yourself look and, of course, did the proper thing. "Come on, guys, back to the bedroom you go," he said, grabbing Fred by the collar and scooping Sampson up under his arm. They departed for the back of the house just as my front doorbell rang.

I jumped up, heedful of my still sore skull and the two glasses of wine I'd polished off. The chief was sitting down again, handing Detective Alston a handkerchief as I walked to my front door. Peering through the peephole, I groaned inwardly. Murphy.

"Open up, Kell, I know you're home, I can hear you shouting from upstairs," he said, his speech already slurred from the glass of Stolichnaya in his hand. He gave the door a loud thump. "Come on, I have a present for you."

What was one more baboon to add to this circus? I opened the door.

"Hey, Murphy, how's it going?"

He walked across the threshold with his glass in one hand and something about two feet tall covered with a towel in the other. He set both down and casually draped his arm around my shoulder and pulled me to him in a hug. Murphy's a fisherman, and tonight he smelled the part, mixed with sweat and Stoli. Ughh. Too close to Murphy.

He looked much as I remembered him from his last visit of two months ago, a tall, lanky frame without one ounce of spare flesh and rough black hair falling past his eyebrows. He had let the back grow out, and it was secured in a loose ponytail. His face was covered in a scraggly beard and mustache, both in desperate need of some sprucing up. Murphy lives on his boat, and is so deeply tanned he could pass as black. Even though he's always been generally pleasant to me, there's something about him that makes me apprehensive, an uneasiness I can't put my finger on. Sure, he drinks too much and cusses too much, but it was more than that. He slunk in and out of town like a restless pirate, usually leaving chaos in his wake. I recoiled involuntarily from his hug, visions of an unknown murderer working on my fragile psyche and wondering exactly when Murphy had arrived. Before the first murder?

"Super, sweetheart, super. Just wait until you see what I've got for you," he replied in a dark, liquid voice tinged with the precise tones of a New Englander. "Hey, what've we got here? A party? Cool, man, cool. Greetings Siobhan, Middleton." Murphy circulated quickly, pumping the chief's hand and then the detective's. "Hey, man, good to meet you, I'm Murphy."

Amused, I watched as the two men gaped at this apparition who had suddenly appeared amongst us. Siobhan waved a hand in greeting while Mid shook hands with Murphy and was awarded with some heavy duty back slapping.

"What's under the towel," I asked, lifting up a corner.

"Yeah, yeah, go ahead, uncover him," Murphy said, flopping down in the spot I'd vacated and draping an arm around Siobhan.

Him? I pulled the towel up over top of a large metal bird cage and was face to face with a large, colorful parrot.

"You have great knockers," said the parrot.

"What? What did you say?" I asked.

"I'm horny. Wanna have sex," asked the parrot.

I whirled around. "Excuse me, Murphy? What is this?"

"It's a parrot, man. Old sea captain friend of mine had him for years, but he's retiring to one of those old fart homes and can't keep him. I know how much you love animals, Kell, so I knew right away he was perfect for you." Murphy beamed.

Siobhan clapped her hands with delight and came over to the cage. "How utterly adorable! What's his name?"

"Blackbeard," Murphy answered. Of course, I thought.

"Why, hello, Blackbeard, what a pretty bird you are," Siobhan leaned over towards the bird.

"Show me your hooters," Blackbeard said.

"Not now, you silly bird, we have company." She giggled, tipping her wine glass in Mid's direction. "Get me a refill, darlin'."

"Siobhan, don't you think you've had enough?" I asked.

"I'm Irish," she replied.

"Well, bully for you." I was beginning to get exasperated. Tires screeched to an abrupt halt outside my house, and a door slammed shut.

"Yoohoo, hello up there! Lights out on the front porch! Sea turtles dig the dark!"

I peered through the curtains. Making her way to my front door was Bonnie McLeod, all sharp angles and jutting jaw firmly leading the way. She was wearing her standard uniform of blue jeans and a white t-shirt topped off with an ancient jean jacket. An unrelentless ball of energy, I could see huge bags of dog and cat food piled high in the back of her silver pick-up truck. This was one lady on a mission to help animals, a point I reminded myself of as I let my head lean against the door. This day was not going to end. I took a deep breath.

"Bonnie," I exclaimed brightly. "How good to see you." She pulled me to her in a bear hug, juggling a shoebox in one hand. Great, more presents.

She looked around my living room, assessing the situation, and was immediately the first lady of Folly. "Good evening, Strom, I believe my husband would like to speak with you about the horrendous council meeting. We simply must have officers on hand next time. The place was in utter turmoil."

Chief Stoney raised a hand in greeting. "Yep, the natives were definitely restless that night," he grunted, folding his arms across his chest.

Bonnie peered down her nose at him for a second, then turned to me. "Kell, my dear, I know you're busy and I won't be but a minute," she said. "I simply have too many orphans to handle right now. Here you go." She thrust the shoebox at me. I carefully lifted the lid.

"Baby squirrels! Oh, Bonnie, they're so tiny. Don't they have to be fed every two hours?" As much as I love nursing all sorts of creatures back to life, I was positive I couldn't handle this tonight.

Siobhan angled over for a view. "I'll handle the wee rats tonight, since I'm staying over."

News to me. But fine with me. I honestly didn't care if the whole lot of them spent the night at this point. I handed the box over to Siobhan and went to the kitchen in search of the wine bottle.

"Can I get you anything, Bonnie," I asked as I walked away.

"No, no, I have to get home to feed everyone. Wherever did you get this lovely parrot?"

"You have great knockers," Blackbeard declared.

"Oh, my," Bonnie replied.

"Wanna have sex?"

By this time I had made it to my kitchen and was spared the rest of the conversation. As I was rooting around in the drawer for the wine opener, Mid appeared. He gently retrieved the opener from my hand, expertly opened another bottle of his vintage merlot, and poured me half a glass.

"Listen, Kell, I told the chief I'd ask you a few questions, or you can tell me what happened this morning, and I'll answer to Alston for tonight. You look like you're ready to fall over," he said.

I glanced out the kitchen door in to the living room where my guests were gathered. The chief and Detective Alston were carrying on a conversation with Murphy, Siobhan was engaged with Bonnie, and Blackbeard was talking to himself.

"They've already talked with Elbie," Mid continued. "So they have his version of the story."

"What was he doing there, anyways?" I asked.

"Says he wanted to go bike riding with you and skipped the bus. His mom had already left for work. He knows you only bike to the east end, so he followed. Says you were asleep when he got there." Mid's warm brown eyes looked troubled.

In less than five minutes I poured my heart out to him, explaining how the girl simply wasn't there, and then about 30 minutes later when I started back, she was. By the time I was finished, I was wiped out and began to nod off.

Mid said, "Siobhan's sleeping in your spare room tonight. I'll escort all your guests out and explain you've gone to bed. I'll take the two men to the Coast for a drink and hash over this, so go to your room." He gave me a quick hug and pushed me in the direction of my bedroom.

I gave him a look of gratitude. "Thanks, Mid."

He shrugged. "What friends are for, right?"

I'd just made it to my door when he spoke again. "Hey, Kell? Listen, don't go for any early morning outings tomorrow, okay?"

Not on your life, I thought.

CHAPTER SEVENTEEN

Sometime in the middle of the night Siobhan woke me up. Snoring alerted me to another presence in my bed and I turned my head. Fred was stretched out perpendicular to me in my queen size bed. I was going to have to get him a video of other dogs sleeping in beds, proving the fact that they can indeed curl up in balls. Fred was maximizing the available space by sticking his tail straight out and allowing his tongue to hang out the other end. Sampson had planted himself between my feet on top of the covers, and between the two of them I was successfully trapped beneath the blankets.

"What is it," I groggily asked, struggling to unwrap myself from my animals.

"Well, I was up feeding the wee ones and your discharge papers say to check on you during the night, so here we are." Siobhan gently placed a baby squirrel on my belly, and it quickly scooted up until he was at my neck and nestled in my hair.

"Hmmm, so sweet. How many are there?"

"Eight, and I'd say they're all going to make it, they're sturdy little fellows." She held another in her hand, letting it suckle on the tiny water dropper filled with formula. Tiny claws pawed at the air. The moonlight coming through my windows played off shiny little eyes, so trusting and alert. They never cease to amaze me, these orphaned creatures who adapt so readily to being handled and fed. The one at my neck nuzzled around in an attempt to make a nest for the night.

Siobhan gathered him from my hair, said goodnight, and left me to my dreams.

Normally, I sleep soundly and mostly dreamlessly, but as I drifted back off it appeared there was a director waiting in the wings to take charge of the show. He plunged me into the darkness, where I felt myself sinking in sand, surrounded by water. I tried to climb out and head for shore, but I was stuck, trapped in pluff mud. My hands got tangled up in seaweed, except it wasn't seaweed, it was hair, blond and wet, pulling floating bodies closer to me. Jennifer Donnelly and Darla Simmons smiled at me, faces bloated with water and eyes mocking. They weren't on surfboards, they were just floating in the ocean, attached to my hands with their hair.

"Help us, Kell. You're the only one who can," whispered Jennifer. Her blue eyes rolled around in her head.

"Please, Kell, help us. Find our killer, Kell," echoed Darla. Her hands were outstretched and there were angry red circles in the palms.

"Go away, both of you! I can't help you, you're already dead!" I tried to untangle my hands from their hair. "Go away!"

"It's you who can solve this, Kell. Help us," implored Jennifer.

I tried in vain to extricate my hands and the hair turned in to snakes, slimy and oozing in the water, wrapping my hands and pinning me to the dead girls. They cackled gleefully. "Help us, Kell, help us." I tried to wake up but the director wouldn't let me.

"What can I do," I screamed in my dream.

"Go surfing, Kell, it's so much fun. For awhile there, it saved my life," giggled Darla. The snakes were starting to lash out at me with their forked tongues and I screamed louder, sobs shaking my body.

The snakes were turning their tongues to my face now, so slimy I could feel them as they attacked. My eyes opened to the sight of Fred sitting up in my bed, a bit too close as he slobbered on my cheeks and howled softly. A dream. "Just a dream, fur face, just a dream." I shivered as I pulled Fred close for a hug. First time in his life he was ever awake before me.

I reached for my glasses, read the clock, and was elated for once to not have to go back to sleep. Ten after seven, the latest I'd slept in a long time. Fred, reassured that I was no longer in any imminent danger, was not having the same sort of morning and was happily slipping back in to inertia. Tonight I'd send him camping back to his own doggie bed. He was really milking this dead body thing for all it was worth.

I puttered in my slippers out to the kitchen, where Siobhan had so kindly made the coffee the night before. She had set it for seven a.m., but no sign of Siobhan. She was most likely worn out from babysitting all night long.

I made my cup and carried it to the living room, going from window to window opening up the white wooden-slat blinds to greet the day. The sun was strong for such an early hour, and I shivered even as the rays streamed inside, dancing around playfully on the walls.

"Poof dream, you're gone," I muttered aloud. "Too much sunshine here for you."

Okay, the dream was gone, but what about the mail? Cautiously, I unlocked my front door and slowly eased it open, poking my head carefully to check for any more letters. Things appeared pretty normal, except for the creature wrapped in a tablecloth of some sort in the front yard, clutching an empty bottle of Stoli. Murphy. He was ranting to the heavens, oblivious of me. I quickly backed inside and closed the door quietly. I made a mental note to ask the chief to run a background check on him. Problem was I didn't know his last name. A chill went up my spine when I realized just how paranoid I'd become.

"Show me your hooters."

I jumped, the coffee in my mug sloshing over the sides. "Shit! Don't sneak up on me like that," I instructed the parrot in the cage. I'd forgotten about Blackbeard.

"Nobody put your towel back on, now you're going to have to sleep during the day," I told him. "Promise to get you back on schedule."

"I want to have sex," he said as I dropped the towel down.

"You're sure a cheeky little bird. What kind of old sea captain raised you, anyway?" I muttered. "I'm going to have to teach you some manners."

I sank down on my couch, tucking my legs up under me and reached for the afghan my mom crocheted for me. She gave it to me for my birthday last year and it always makes me feel close to her. I pulled it around my shoulders, shivering, and sipped my coffee. My dream rattled around in my head.

"Morning," mumbled Siobhan from the kitchen. She came out with a mug in one hand and the shoebox of squirrels in the other, her hair a mass of curly red tangles hanging down her back.

"Morning," I replied.

She plugged an electric heating pad in a socket and set the box on top of it. Squirrels get cold fairly easily. "These furry fellows are great birth control." She yawned, stretching her arms above her head. "Imagine having an infant and getting up at all ungodly hours just to feed the thing."

Siobhan sat down on the floor next to the box and regarded me with knowing green eyes. "Didn't sleep, did you," she asked, crossing her legs.

"Actually, I did," I said.

"Well, you don't look like your usually cheery self, although I can certainly understand that, finding another dead girl and all."

Gee, thanks for the compassion, I thought. I pulled my afghan closer around my shoulders and sighed. "I did have this sort of wacky dream."

Siobhan brightened. She is seriously in tune with the dream world, claiming it's our subconscious at work offering glimpses into the portals of our brains. Me, I pay no attention to what my brain does while I sleep, I've got enough trouble keeping up with it in my waking hours. This dream, however, had made me sit up and take notice.

"Go on, I'm listening," Siobhan instructed.

I rehashed my dream, describing the awful snakes and the pleas from Jennifer and Darla. Siobhan nodded encouragingly, her eyes shining with excitement. When I got to the part where Darla told me to go surfing, Siobhan paled visibly.

"She said what? Exactly what did she say, Kell?" she whispered.

"She told me to go surfing, it was fun," I said.

"No, say it like you did the first time," she whispered urgently.

I thought a minute. "Well, she said 'go surfing, it's so much fun and it saved my life for a while.' Something like that."

Siobhan got up and began to pace the floor. I watched her a few seconds. "What?" I couldn't take it anymore. "What is it?"

She paused dramatically midstride and looked me in the eyes. "Did you ever meet Darla Simmons?"

My town is small, but even I don't know everyone. "Nope, never met her."

"After you went to bed last night Bonnie left, she wants you to call her, by the way. We kicked Murphy out, and Mid tried to leave with the other two, but as I was stuck here with you, I couldn't tag along," Siobhan began. I stuck my tongue out at her.

"I whipped up another pot of coffee and doused everyone's mug with a hearty helping of Bailey's, and that pretty much convinced them to stay. I wasn't getting left out of the loop," she explained.

"You used my Bailey's? I was saving that for ice cream," I protested.

"Guess what? I slipped 'em some of your rum, too. Really loosened their tongues." Siobhan grinned.

Despite myself I was proud of her. Nasty Detective Alston deserved it, and Chief Stoney was forever yelling at me. "So here's where we are. The murders are definitely related, the killer used the same type of boat rope to secure the bodies to the surfboards. Both girls had on identical purple rash guards. Remind me what your favorite color is again, Kell," she paused.

"You know my favorite color."

"Bollocks, would you play along here."

"Okay, purple, but that's just a coincidence," I argued weakly.

"Anyway, Jennifer was 19, Darla was 21, both blondes with similar features, both around 5'4" or so and both pretty athletic." She looked me over. Suddenly I didn't feel so great. "Here's the difference. Jennifer had been dead less then 24 hours when you found her, while Darla had expired at least a week earlier, according to what they've been able to determine so far."

A week ago? "How can that be? Wouldn't she have been, you know......"

"Decomposed? Exactly. Whoever killed her kept her body on ice somehow. She was quite nicely preserved. Cause of death, strangulation, same as Jennifer, but Darla looked like she'd been, um, tortured beforehand." Siobhan grimaced.

I knew I shouldn't ask, but hey, I'm a reporter. Curiosity and all that.

"Tortured? How?"

Siobhan shook her hair back off her face, plopped down next to me on the couch and snagged a corner of my afghan. She pulled it around her shoulders.

"It's creepy, Kell. She had these puncture wounds in her palms, like from nails or something and her back was covered in welts, like from a belt."

My breathing stopped. "Like in my dream."

"You say welts on her back in your dream?"

"No, I saw these marks on her hands."

Siobhan shook her head. "Your internal consciousness is speaking to you, Kell. Get this. One of the officer's thought he recognized Darla and even knew where she lived. You know those little cottages on the west end, the ones old Mr. Roland rents out?"

I nodded in agreement, not trusting my voice.

"They brought poor Mr. Roland in to identify the body. Sure enough, he rented to her. Said she had lived there roughly two years, showed up one day beaten up pretty badly by her ex-boyfriend and strung out on crack. Had some money, told Mr. Roland she was determined to clean up. He felt sorry for her and let her take a place," Siobhan continued. "They were fairly close, and she confided in him that surfing had literally saved her life, made her strong."

I jumped to my feet. "Quit making stuff up, Siobhan, you're giving me the creeps."

She cocked her head to one side, acknowledging my doubt. "About time you appreciated the power of your dreams. Your dead girls are speaking to you from beyond, Kell. Not a wise idea to ignore them. They'll only get louder."

It was my turn to pace. I listened with a vague sense of unreality. My life was careening away out of my control, but I knew with pulse-pounding certainty she was right.

"Fine, I'll listen to them," I cried, my hands balled in fists at my side. "Just what exactly am I supposed to do?"

Siobhan unfolded her long legs and stood up, put her hands on my shoulders and peered down at me.

"Come on. We're going surfing."

CHAPTER EIGHTEEN

We were cruising past the washout, Siobhan at the wheel of my Four-Runner and me in the passenger seat. She slowed down, offering me an eyeful of my destiny. Blue-white ripples in the water glistened in the sun, and the sky glared hot, with only a few scribbles of clouds visible. I watched as surfers took off on waves, some heading right, others left, emitting whoops of war-cries as they skated impossibly fast across the ocean's surface. We idled there a moment, observing as some of the surfers high-fived it after an apparently successful ride. This was a clan, I decided, one I was not quite sure I wanted to belong to.

Surfing wasn't brand new to me, thanks to the few months I spent with Fletcher during my senior year in college. He had convinced me to paddle out with him on several occasions, and although all I ever really did was sit out in the water spending time with him, I did attempt a few take-offs of my own. My surfing experience culminated with the last fateful ride that brought my board crashing down on my skull. Fletcher told me to shake it off, but the blood pouring out of my right ear seemed rather important. The emergency room doctors agreed.

When we reached Center Street, Siobhan parked in front of Jonah's Surf Shop across the street from the Coast. I'd been in here one time before, a few years ago to interview the elderly gentleman who'd launched the shop back in the '60's. We got out and climbed the stairs.

"Now, remember, Alex gave us the day off so you could stay in bed and I could play nurse maid, so if you see her here anywhere, hide," Siobhan instructed.

We opened the door. Loud, head banging music assaulted me, keeping time to the surf video currently playing on the big screen television set. Beautiful Hawaiian flowers covered the walls and clothes of every shade of the rainbow were artfully displayed beneath bamboo tikis. My impeccably dressed, conservative editor in here? I don't think so.

We made for the counter. "We'd like to rent two surfboards, please," Siobhan informed the tattooed fellow in charge. I stared at him. He was almost as colorful as the clothes, with tattoos racing up and down each arm. His head was shaved bald and he had a long, braided goatee dangling from his chin. He stared back.

"We have shortboards, longboards and funshapes. What'll it be?"

"Funshapes," I blurted. With a name like that, they had to be, well, fun, right?

"Forty bucks each for half the day, sixty each for the whole day, and we close at 6 p.m.," tattoo man stated.

Siobhan whipped out a credit card. "We'll also be requiring lessons. You do teach here, correct?" Lessons. Oh, goody. Maybe our instructor would be one of those heavenly bronzed beach gods. Maybe this wouldn't be so bad, after all.

"Forty bucks for a group lesson, let me go see if we have someone around." He vanished through a door behind the counter.

Siobhan whistled while I glanced around the shop, bursting at the seams with surfing paraphernalia. We had our choices of several brands of surf wax, all guaranteed to keep you glued to your board. Leashes, deck pads, fins, nose guards, roof racks, stickers, watches and sunglasses completed the menu of everything a surfer could possibly need. A sneak at a price tag on a pair of shades made me whistle, too. Not cheap.

Our colorful helper emerged from behind the door with a tiny female. Her mop of short brown hair just about matched her honey brown skin. Six silver studs marched up one earlobe, but the other was bare. Her long neck curved like a bird taking wing, and when she turned around I saw a bright yellow sun tattooed on the back of it. Her eyes were the most unusual shade of violet, with thick, sooty lashes.

"This here's Trista, she's got time for a lesson," said the counter guy.

Trista gave us an elf-like grin, and Siobhan and I both stared down at her curiously. This itty-bitty thing was going to teach us to surf? She couldn't weigh more than 90 pounds soaking wet. Where was my bronzed beach boy?

"Sounds good, ring it up and bring the boards out this way," Siobhan commanded. We turned for the front door.

A laugh brought us up short. "Uh uh, girlfriends, you gotta pull your own weight," Trista said, her voice a surprising throaty rumble. "The boards are back here."

I was already exhausted from lugging around a 7'6" bright blue funshape by the time Siobhan and I followed Trista in her yellow VW Volkswagen back to the washout. We parked behind her and sat, awaiting instructions. She jumped out of her car, motioning us to exit our vehicle. Logical place to start. I let out the breath I was holding.

"Well darlin', here goes nothing," Siobhan exclaimed a bit too excitedly for my liking. She hopped out and went to the back window, pulling out her selection, an 8' red funshape with a star emblazoned on the deck. "Get it in gear, Kell, you're wasting our hour up."

Sounded good to me. Maybe I could just sit here and observe, sort of learn through osmosis. Trista was heading towards the beach, with a board resembling a potato chip grasped under one arm. "Come on, chickabiddies, the waves are calling," she barked like an angry drill instructor. I snapped to attention in my seat. She sure was loud for such a diminutive thing. So much for my osmosis technique.

Reluctantly, I climbed out, tugged on the cumbersome apparatus in the back of my vehicle, and attempted to position it under my arm, Trista style. Even with it shoved up far in to my armpit, my fingers barely reached the edge.

"Okay, you beast. On my head," I said, hoisting it up and balancing it. Everything was fine until I started walking, then it began sliding around precariously. No way was this monster getting the better of me.

"Stay still," I ordered it, tightening my grip. By the time I arrived at the spot Trista and Siobhan had dropped their boards in the sand, I was huffing and my fingers hurt.

"Sheesh, this thing is a pain in the rear," I panted, landing in the sand beside Siobhan. I looked over at Trista. "How come you get such a little one?"

Her uniquely colored eyes twinkled with amusement. "Sister, you'd never be able to balance on this baby," she said, stroking her shortboard lovingly. "Funshapes are for beginners, they're at least 7' and go to 8', rounded with a lot of meat to them. Makes it easier to float."

Fine, you carry it, I thought. I bit my tongue. Mustn't anger the instructor, she'd probably drown me on purpose.

"Okay, first things first. Stand up," Trista ordered. We stood. "It's important to limber up before heading in the water. The ocean is very unforgiving on our spinal chords if you find yourself falling wrong."

"Well, teach us to fall right, then," Siobhan requested. I nodded in agreement.

Trista chuckled, and began leading us through a series of stretches suspiciously resembling yoga moves.

"Is this yoga? Because I don't like yoga," I asked, contorted.

"Yeah, I teach part-time," Trista answered.

I rolled my eyes at Siobhan, who seemed oblivious to my unhappiness. Her hair fell in a long braid down her back, and she actually seemed to be enjoying herself. I pulled my own wayward mane back in to a ponytail and secured it with the scrunchy on my wrist.

"Now, lie down on your boards like this." Trista demonstrated. We complied.

"Okay, jump to your feet and land like this, legs a comfortable distance apart and lead with whichever leg feels right." She hopped nimbly and posed, crouched down like a sumo wrestler.

We jumped. Hey, this wasn't so bad. Down again on our bellies, jump up again to our feet. This went on for several minutes, until Trista was suitably satisfied we had the swing of it.

"All right, get in position, noticing which leg is back. Now reach for your leash and secure it to your trailing leg like this." She pulled the velcro apart and wrapped it around her ankle. We copied.

"Let's go! The waves are perfect for you two today, about one to two feet and glassy, not much of a current," Trista remarked as we walked in to the water. I felt like a pig being led to slaughter. If I lived through this never, ever, would I make fun of Fred again.

"Set your boards down in the water and walk out as far as you can, about waist deep. I'll show you how to duck dive, but you can't do that on a funshape, you just grab the board and go over the top of the wave," our cheerful instructor instructed.

Siobhan and I waded out, trailing behind Trista as she suddenly hopped on her board and paddled towards the oncoming wave. Quick as a flash she was gone, gracefully pushing the nose of her board through the wave, the foot with the leash on it poking up as she disappeared.

We threw our monstrosities over the top of the cresting swell, jumping on the slippery things. We'd waxed them up during breaks in our stretching session, but I must have missed a spot or two. Siobhan paddled out to where Trista sat serenely on her board, and I stroked fast. No way was I getting left behind out here.

"Okay, now sit up and balance yourselves on your boards," Trista said.

Siobhan went first, easing up off her belly until she was upright and straddled the board. "Wow, this sucker is wide. Good thing my leg muscles are strong from riding Jupiter. I could crush this baby like a nut," she said.

Siobhan has a beautiful palomino she boards at a stable on John's Island. "Yeah, crush it and it'll run you about three-hundred bucks to replace, since it's used and all," Trista said.

Smart aleck. I swung my body up, grabbing the sides of the board until I was sitting, and the finicky thing shot right out between my legs, flipping me backwards. Salty sea water got up my nose and I came up sputtering and coughing to the sounds of laughter.

"Very funny," I snorted.

Trista controlled herself. "You have to stay in the middle of the board."

We did this for a while, practicing the fine art of sitting still while floating in the ocean. Not as easy as it looks, I might add. I'd mastered the technique the summer with Fletcher, and was determined to at least get the sitting still part right again. During this time Trista would occasionally shout, "I'm gonna take this one, be right back," and pop up on her potato chip, expertly maneuvering it this way and that over the wave's face.

"That's called going down the line," she explained, paddling back and shaking her head, sprays of water glistening in the sun. "When you first start out, the tendency is to ride the wave straight in. The real fun begins when you can steer."

"Hey, Trista, what's up," greeted a tow-headed guy in a black rash guard as he paddled by.

"Harley, what's up?" she responded.

He stopped mid-paddle and idled next to us. I recognized him as one of the surfers from the Starfish. Siobhan and I looked at each other, eyebrows raised.

"Some sick shit going on. Did you hear about that Darla chick?" Harley asked.

"Yeah, I heard. I didn't know her too well, but it's weird, right after Jenny. Wonder who in the world would hurt them." Trista shivered in the water.

"What happened," I asked, all wide-eyed innocence. I was out here for a reason, and my reporting skills were in high gear, or maybe it was my new-found investigative streak. Dead girls told me to do this, and I wasn't taking it lightly.

Harley looked Siobhan and me over, glancing questioningly at Trista.

"Lesson," she said.

He must have found this an acceptable excuse to finding two new faces in his playground. "One of our friends was killed a couple of days ago, and then this other girl was, too. Both surfers."

Siobhan and I made big saucer eyes at him. "You don't say," she said.

"It's true. We've kinda got this theory it could be another surfer doing it," Harley said.

"You're kidding. Why do you think that?" I asked, glancing around. Time to pay attention to the others floating around out here.

Harley grabbed a gelatinous blob near his fingertips and lobbed it at Trista.

"Yuck, jelly balls, " she shrieked, lobbing it back at him.

"No exact theory, just something from the gut, you know? A bunch of us talked about it, and we, like, just feel it," Harley explained. He laughed self-consciously. "You probably don't think we're that bright, but we do have good intuition. Comes from knowing which waves to take off on and which ones to pass up."

Siobhan spoke up excitedly. "Do you believe in the power of your dreams?"

Oh, for heaven's sake, we'd be holding a séance out here if these two kept it up. Trista looked interested, and the three of them embarked on a conversation I tuned out. I looked around.

People were spread out from one end of the washout to the other. All ages, from what I could see, and a surprising number of females. When I had been out here five years ago with Fletcher, women were an obvious minority. Now it appeared they'd taken to the water in droves, easily rivaling their male counterparts in numbers and seriously showing them up when it came to fashion.

There was a group of girls a little ways down from us, laughing and cavorting with the crowd of guys circling them like sharks. I sat on my board, unabashedly spying. I pegged them as teenagers, all brown-skinned and bleached hair, sporting bikinis so skimpy I wondered how they stayed put when they surfed, if they actually were out here in the Atlantic to catch waves. One girl was on her belly with a thong wedged in place, bare buttocks soaking up the rays while she idly splashed the water with her hands. Okay, here was a serious surfer. No way was that thing staying on if she wiped out. One flaxen-haired girl caught my attention, and I paddled closer. Yep, Beau's daughter Cristina.

"Hey, Cristina, how's it going?" I asked casually, like it was no big deal I was out at sea clinging to a piece of fiberglass.

Cristina held her hand up to shield the sun and get a better look at who was intruding on teenager time. The four or five other girls and handful of guys all fixed me with closed expressions as I edged my way closer.

"Oh, hi. Kell, I, um, didn't recognize you," Cristina said, her infectious grin a duplicate of her daddy's. Silky hair hung down her back in a wet stream stopping just short of the pink bikini bottoms held in place by strings on each side. I hadn't seen Cristina in a while, not since she sprouted a chest. The freckles splattered across her nose were practically all that was left of the child she used to be.

"Gee Cristina, you've grown up! What grade are you in?" I asked.

"Um, I'm graduating this year," she said, paddling over to me. The rest of the group quickly lost interest and were back to their horsing around. Reminded me of surfing with Fletcher and his friends. I used to sit out here like that, goofing off and imagining myself looking quite the beach babe. Hey, at least I never wore a thong.

"So, how's this work out here," I joked. "Are there any groups, or gangs, or what?" Cristina gave me a puzzled look, then her eyes lit up as the smile spread across her face.

"Oh, you mean, like surfers? That's funny, but pretty true, I guess, I mean, there are different people that hang together," she replied. We surveyed the scene.

"So what do you call that group?" I nodded towards a pack of long boarders sitting a bit further out in the water. I squinted. Sure enough, Judge Brooks's shiny bald head was soaking up a few rays of its own.

Cristina made a face, scrunching up her eyes. "Old," she said.

I laughed, surprised at her lack of manners. "Hey, watch it, child, I've got a few years on you, too."

She made a display of pulling herself up off her belly so she was straddling the board. It really did look easy when she did it. Maybe I had more years on her than I'd admit to. While I was admiring this show of youthful flexibility, Cristina let out a most unladylike spit which landed in the ocean with a plop.

"And that," she said. "Is what I think of that old fart." Okay, so Beau's daughter had definitely grown up, what with the spitting and all. She adjusted her pink bikini top. Of course, there was the chest, too.

"You mean Brooks? Wow, I thought it was just me," I said.

"He's a dirty old pervert, always trying to look at my butt when I paddle by. Plus, he's threatened Daddy," Cristina replied, still glaring in the direction of Brooks and his equally elderly surfing companions.

Hmmm, gossiping while at sea. I might have to hang out in the water more often, might get some good story ideas. "Threatened your dad how?"

"Not sure exactly, just what I heard when Daddy was on the phone with him, something about how he voted," she answered, looking over towards her group of playmates.

Preston Brooks was certainly making enemies fast these days. "How about those people over there?" Might as well get to know the players out here while I could.

"Them? They're posers, wannabes, you know. Have all the money, buy all the right stuff, but can't surf," she snorted, glancing in the direction of a few others out in the noon day sun.

A lone paddler headed towards the aforementioned group, turning to give me a quick glance. In that instant, I felt a whisper of terror run through me. Despite the warm sun, I felt chilled, and all my internal warning systems went off at once.

"Except her," Cristina continued, unaware of my sudden fear. "She's kind of like their ring leader, 'cept she can surf okay. She's kinda old compared to the rest of the posers, but all those rich snobs stick together, ya know?"

Drat if Ms. Ring Leader didn't give me goose bumps, plus she looked vaguely familiar. "What's her name?"

"Chelsea Chester, I always think it sounds like a rabbit, so I remember it. She moved away for a while and just got back to town a few months ago. Loaded to the hilt." Cristina shrugged her shoulders, then eased back down on her board. "Hey, Kell, I gotta get back to my buds, okay," she said, paddling away.

I barely heard her bid me farewell. Chelsea Chester. Cuddly little rabbit my ass. Definitely a bit older than the others she was with because I graduated from college with her myself. She had done her dandiest to befriend me when we met on the track team, then split up my friendship with Siobhan, and finally horn in on Fletcher. I'd tried to like her, really I had, but she was strangely obsessive and controlling. Siobhan swears she tried to poison her lunch one of the times we ate with her in the cafeteria, but we chalked it up to the egg salad. Fletcher's head got bigger than normal with all the attention Chelsea flung his way, until he was positive she tried to run him down with her Porsche. I hadn't seen her in years, yet I could hear her rat-a-tat-tat laughter over the crashing waves as if it were yesterday. I turned my board around and paddled back to tell Siobhan the news.

"Hey, guess who that is." I pointed towards the quickly departing figure of Chelsea Chester as I reached the trio.

My water buddies were deeply involved with some heavy philosophical ponderings and ignored me. "Listen up!" I shouted at them.

They stared at me in surprise. "What?" asked Harley.

"See that person paddling away, way down there?"

"Where?" they all asked at once, craning their necks in the direction I was pointing.

"There, there," I yelled as the figure got swallowed up by the throngs in the ocean. I scrambled to my feet and tried to stand up on my board. Bad idea. My arms propelled out in either direction as I felt my board wobble beneath me. I was performing a dance that would make James Brown look like a white guy when I shot overboard, the water taking the full weight of my body as I splashed down.

CHAPTER NINETEEN

Later in the day, my illustrious performance upon a surfboard a comfortable distance behind me, I sat in the sand across the street from my house. An ice-cold Corona complete with two lime wedges was nestled in the koozie I clutched in one hand and I had a Frisbee in the other. I held it under Fred's nose, launching it towards the gray-green gloom of the ocean. We watched it together as it landed near the shoreline. I'd been trying to teach Fred to play Frisbee for a while now, but he wasn't getting the hang of it.

Over my shoulder, the sun was dropping over the marsh, streaking the sky with brilliant hues of purple and orange, determined to put on one last display before saying good-night. Rough sea winds swept like lost souls searching for release, whipping my hair and stinging my eyes. I sipped my beer and listened to the waves crash fiercely on the sand, only to retreat with a whisper as the tide gathered the water up so it could do it again. This repetitive cycle normally soothes me, but memories of actually being out in the midst of the mighty deep gave me a different take on the serene seas. I'd seen plenty of people tossed like rag dolls today. Siobhan had attempted a take off and was immediately punished by the churning wave. She compared it to how clothes must feel like in a washing machine.

Her reaction to Chelsea appearing on Folly was one of unrestrained mirth. She laughed so hard she fell off her board, and could barely control herself when I relayed my feelings of misgiving. Her words went something like "that snooty psycho who impersonated you and fooled around with Fletcher here at Folly?" She then entertained our new buddies Trista and Harley with stories which made Chelsea sound exactly like Dr. Jekyll and Mr. Hyde. I'd forgotten some of them, and I shivered and pulled my jacket tighter against the now howling winds. Maybe ol'Chelsea Chester would just blend right in with the rest of the eccentrics in town and I wouldn't even notice her.

I watched the dark come, dusting the night ash orange. Out at sea, way beyond the breaking waves, a lone boat crept along, lights illuminating the water. Even in the dark I felt exposed somehow, and huddled closer to Fred. The approaching sounds of someone singing "yo ho, yo ho, it's a pirate's life for me" broke the silence.

Murphy and Ludmilla strolled along the water's edge, spotting Fred and me where we sat. I sighed. I really wasn't in the mood for company.

"Evening, Kell! What a glorious night! Can't you feel the storm brewing," bellowed Ludmilla. Murphy kept up his off-tune melody.

"Hey, y'all," I replied. "Yeah, I feel it. There's a hurricane forming out there, still too far away to worry about." Although this was not quite the end of May and the Atlantic hurricane season runs from June until the end of September, sometimes they'll pop up slightly off season. I'd become a bit jaded over the years waiting with each storm to see if we'd be evacuated. That was one fiasco I simply was not up to right about now.

Ludmilla peered at me in the darkness. "Sit up straight, Kell. Your spine will thank you, remember. You look a bit peaked. Come to think of it, so did Elbert after that horrible incident with your dead girl."

Everyone was determined to assign them to me. I gave up. I looked out at the ocean. The boat I'd seen was crawling by, barely visible by the light of the new moon.

I pointed. "Murphy, what kind of boat is that?"

Murphy squinted in the darkness. "Hard to see real well, but looks like about a forty-foot cruiser. Not bad." He whistled. "Those babies aren't cheap."

Murphy lives on a single-engine fishing trawler, traveling up and down the coast from Cape Cod to Florida, fishing and cavorting as he pleases. He keeps his Cadillac parked at the Maritime Marina on Folly, where he docks his boat when he's in town. I'd often wondered if he had a car and a Ludmilla in every port. The two of them sat down next to Fred and me in the sand.

"How's Elbie doing, Ludmilla?" I asked.

Ludmilla gave a toss of her platinum ringlets, sending them jiggling all over her head like tiny slinkys. "Well, it was one heck of a day at the police station yesterday. That little fellow with the giant glasses was determined to make an example out of poor Elbert, but Chief Stoney let me bring him home, no charges," she answered. "The chief said he'd take the matter up with you."

Well, of course he would, now wouldn't he? Mayhem just seemed to cling to me like barnacles lately. Who would blame the chief?

Murphy reached back and pulled the elastic securing his long, inky hair, and the wind immediately whipped it around his head like a whirling black dervish. "Ah, nothing like a little salt air to clear the mind," he remarked through the cloud of now tangled strands. He cleared his throat and peered intently at me. "So, Kell, what do you make of these murders? Guess I showed up just in time for all the action, huh?"

I met his gaze, drained my beer, and turned the bottle upside down in the sand. "Yeah, guess so."

"But really, it is very strange, we don't have crime here on Folly," Ludmilla interjected. "Well, of course, we have the normal crimes, drunk and disorderly and growing marijuana in backyards and such, but murder? I've never heard of it."

Gee, I hope nobody ever interviewed Ludmilla for an article on life at the beach. "It's odd, I agree, and no suspects that I've heard of yet." I gauged Murphy's reaction to my statement. He put a protective arm around Ludmilla's broad shoulders.

"Well, neither of you should worry your pretty little heads over it, not while I'm in town. Any murderer comes messin' around my women will deal with this," he pronounced, reaching under his jeans near the ankle and unsheathing a small, curved blade that caught the moonlight.

I flinched and looked at Fred. Nope, wasn't bothering him. He was snoring.

"Oh, my love, will you put that awful thing away! You're scaring Kell," admonished Ludmilla.

Murphy complied. "Aye, mateys, I'm just an old pirate, remember." He launched in to another round of yo ho's, pulling Ludmilla down in the sand as he shrieked with laughter.

"Enough for me, I'm heading home. Up, Fred. Bye, folks," I said, pulling Fred to his feet by his collar, which was rather difficult while he was asleep, but I wasn't sitting out here in the dark while a murderer prowled my town. Especially not with Murphy. Fred was alert enough for us to scramble over the dunes, look both ways, and crossed the street.

I changed in to some comfy sweats, took out my contacts and scrubbed my face. I grabbed another Corona from the fridge and shoved two slices in it, turning the bottle upside down and plugging it with my thumb. The limes sank to the bottom in slow motion. Fred waited, and I turned the bottle upright, letting my thumb out and gave him a little squirt of beer. He held his tongue out and expertly caught the drops.

I made a tuna fish sandwich and went to the living room, plopping down on the couch and turning on the television set. Fred stretched out on his doggie bed and began to snore, so I turned the volume up a bit. The ocean crashed across the street, the wind moaning intrusively, so I turned the volume up a little more. Elbie began to shout upstairs, "......so you better watch your balls, Murphy, cause I got an exacto knife and I ain't afraid to use it.....", so I turned the volume up again. By this time the television was so loud I couldn't hear myself think, which was fine by me. I felt like my mind had hung out a Do Not Disturb sign.

I downed my beer and finished my dinner, stretched out on the couch and tried to concentrate on the movie I'd landed on. My inner thighs were sore from clutching the surfboard between them all morning, and my head was woozy from my Coronas. I felt myself drifting off, welcoming the peace. But alas, the director was there, lurking in the shadows of my mind.

"Kell, come on in, the water's warm," Jennifer Donnelly beckoned, reaching out a soggy hand.

Darla Simmons stretched her colorless hands towards me, palms up. "You know, this really makes me mad. Being dead sucks as it is, but I have to look at these ugly marks, too." Her inflamed hands reached for me.

Through the hazy murk I felt them touching me, cold and persistent. "Come swim, Kell, join us," their voices echoed in my head.

"Leave me alone, don't touch me," I screamed. "What do you want?"

Their laughter tinkled and they floated in the water. A small fish swam out of Jennifer's mouth while she giggled and a hermit crab crawled out of Darla's nose. I shrank back, but they wouldn't leave. I was in the water now, with the two of them splashing happily around me.

"I did what you said, I went surfing. What can I do," I whimpered.

The two dead girls continued to drift around me, buoyant and blissful. "It's all about the water, Kell," Jennifer whispered and suddenly I was swimming, too, bobbing up and down with my two water-logged companions. They circled me, moving so swiftly they seemed to merge into one.

"You'll find the answers in the water," Darla agreed. "Hurry up, or you'll be one of us."

"No," I screamed. "Get away from me!"

They laughed crazily, sea creatures emerging from various orifices. Jennifer's eyes rolled back in her head and she reached out with arms like tentacles and grabbed my shoulders, drawing me close so I could see the welts on her neck. "Better yet, Kell, just forget about us and before you know it, you'll be with us forever."

"Stop it, let go of me!"

The two girls stopped splashing and rose up out of the water, hovering a moment in thin air.

"Hurry up, Kell, or we'll all be together soon," they said as one.

CHAPTER TWENTY

My eyes were gritty from my restless night as I drove along East Ashley in the early morning summer storm. The clouds were cold, white ghostly mists floating aimlessly in the sky, and the rain streaked past my windshield like tears. I gave the washout a suspicious sideways squint as I passed by, waiting for the killer to throw himself in my path.

I'd been on the phone with Alex all morning going over the murders and was now on my way to meet with Chief Stoney for yet another exciting update. My shoulders slumped forwards over the steering wheel. Why me, I moaned, full of self pity. If my brother could see me now he'd die of embarrassment. The Palevacs are not known for their inner sorrows. I squared my shoulders. I could handle this. Besides, someone had to or I'd be joining my dream partners in their watery grave, according to the dead girls. And dead men tell no lies, right? Or is it tales? I shook my head to dislodge them from my mind.

I trotted up the stairs to the police station, waving once again to Marjorie and wishing I was going to see her to get minutes from a council meeting instead of meeting with the chief. I wanted my life back. "At least you still have a life," Darla's voice echoed in my head. "Shut up," I said to her.

"Excuse me," asked Sandra Crull from the dispatcher's chair. She's a large woman, and looked ready to use force if necessary.

"No, not you Sandra, sorry, just talking to myself," I twittered nervously. This really had to stop, I am not the twittering type. "Um, I have an appointment with the chief."

She buzzed me in. "Go on in to his office, he's expecting you."

Well, this was new. A warm welcome. What was the chief up to now? I walked to his open door and the inhaled cigarette smoke drifting out into the hallway.

Chief Stoney sat behind his desk, feet up and smoke rings encircling his balding head. He motioned me inside. "Close the door, Ms. Palevac, would you please."

He brought his legs down to the floor and stood up, pacing back and forth in front of me while I sat at attention, pencil poised. My eyes drifted over the pitiful beasts displayed on his walls, avoiding the fish. I'd had enough sea life in my dream last night.

The chief stopped so abruptly I jumped in my seat. The nervousness in my chest was beginning to annoy me. "So, I understand you did not know either of the victims, is that right, Ms. Palevac?"

"Right."

"And they just appeared in your path, right?"

"Right."

"And your favorite color is purple, right?"

"Right."

"And you are somehow related to one Elbert Dubrov who lists his address as yours, right?"

"Right," I said. "No, I mean wrong. He's my neighbor, he lives upstairs with his mom." This was getting confusing and I was getting angry. I stood up and paced along side of the chief.

"Chief Stoney, please believe me, neither Elbie nor I had anything to do with that girl, or the first one. Don't you have any leads? What about the letter?"

We stopped, facing each other, eye to eye. The chief ran his hands through the tufts of gray at the sides of his head. He sighed.

"Sit down, Kell," he said, easing himself into his own chair. "No, no leads, this is a complete mystery. There are no fingerprints to go by, the killer must wear gloves. The only thing we have is the same half-inch thick boat rope, and the fact that both victims were strangled."

"Where was Darla from originally?" I asked, needing some more facts for my article.

"Chatham County, Georgia. No living relatives except a great-aunt, nobody to miss her either there or here. She was a loner, apparently. Hadn't even been reported missing," said the chief, crushing out his cigarette in the brass moose head ashtray on his desk.

We talked a bit more, and I promised him I'd fax him a copy of my article before it went to press, something I never do, but this was not my area of expertise. I wasn't about to argue with the authorities.

I waved good-bye to Sandra as I left, and she glanced at me out of the corner of her eye while she answered the phone, giving a half-hearted wave. The clunky brown clogs I was wearing clomped on the floor in a rather unflattering manner, so I stepped things up a bit as I made it down the empty hallway. This only produced echoing thumps that made it sound like someone was following me, so I took the shoes off and carried them, scooting outside in my bare feet. I'd parked right out front and I threw the shoes in my car first, then jumped in after them, barely escaping a few raindrops.

A sudden tap on my windshield made me jump as if I'd been pinched. A bright orange poncho flapped in the rain, obscuring the face of its owner. The wind settled for a moment and Cyrus' large, dome-shaped head appeared for a second as he struggled to keep the billowing plastic from engulfing him once again. He tapped louder.

I rolled my window down. "What's up Cyrus? You look like a giant pumpkin."

He grinned as the water trickled off his smooth scalp. "Not too many people allowed to talk at me that way, darlin'. Here, this was on your windshield and as it was starting to rain, I nabbed it for ya." He thrust a rumpled white envelope through my half opened window, and before my brain registered I took it from him. My name, once again spelled out in mismatched, cut-out letters, loomed before me.

"Shit," I shrieked, dropping the thing in my lap.

Cyrus tried to stick his head in the window. "What's wrong, there a spider or somethin'?"

I fished around in the glove box and found a napkin, with which I gingerly retrieved the menacing object, got out of my car, and secured a portion of the poncho covering Cyrus. Thus partially protected from the drizzle, I walked back to the entrance to City Hall, forcing Cyrus along with me.

"Hey, where we goin', I ain't goin' in the po-lice station, wouldja slow down a minute," he complained. I kept walking, opened the door and pulled him through with me. I held the envelope at arms length.

"Okay, Cyrus, where did this come from?"

He looked around as a few people passed us by and tried to pull his poncho out of my grasp. I held tight, and he began to whine in a very un-Kojak like fashion.

"I don't like it in here, what are we doin' here, it ain't good for me to be seen hanging out here," Cyrus moaned.

It was all I could do to resist slapping him upside the head. Okay, so he had issues with City Hall. Probably every biker slash bouncer slash red-blooded Confederate rabblerouser had issues with City Hall, but I had no time for sympathy. Time to call in the reinforcements. We set off in the direction of the police department.

"Hey, I know where you're takin' me, Kell, why're we goin' this way," Cyrus whined, dragging his feet. I glanced down at my own feet. Shoot, I was barefoot, having made such a hasty exit from my vehicle. I hoped the chief didn't notice.

Sandra Crull glanced up from the telephone and gave the two of us the once over. "Call you back, looks like the great pumpkin has arrived," she said, disconnecting. "May I help you?"

"Yes, please tell the chief I'm back again and need to see him right away," I yanked on the poncho as Cyrus made movements towards the door. "It's urgent."

Sandra buzzed us in and we stood in the small waiting area while she let Chief Stoney know we were there. "Yuck, Cyrus, this poncho is soaked. Take it off and let it dry for a bit," I said.

Cyrus complied, having by now accepted whatever odd fate he felt had befallen him on this strange outing. He hung the poncho on the coat rack in the corner near the door. Underneath, he had on a black t-shirt that read "Legalize It" over a giant marijuana leaf, topped off with his well-worn black leather jacket featuring a giant Confederate flag on the back. Black jeans and worn black boots completed his outfit.

Strom Stoney stood in his doorway, arms folded across his chest. I grasped the evidence tightly and held it out towards him. Turning around he went back in his office, and Sandra motioned us in the same direction with a toss of her head. I grabbed Cyrus by the arm, ignoring his mutterings, and followed the chief back to the smoke-filled place.

He was sitting behind his desk already with his hands folded together in front of him. Still holding the envelope, I sat in a chair and told Cyrus to take the other one.

"I don't want to sit," he pouted.

"Cyrus, sit down," I said.

"No way, then Chief will start askin' me all sorts of questions and I ain't got answers, so no way," Cyrus huffed.

I was beginning to loose patience, and apparently so was the chief as we both barked "Sit down" in unison. Cyrus sat.

I dropped the envelope on the desk. "This was on my windshield."

Chief Stoney eyed the envelope, then Cyrus. "And he is with us because?"

"The hell if I know," Cyrus shouted, jumping to his feet.

"Sit down!" I shouted, grabbing his arm.

Officer Adams stuck his head in the half-closed door. "Need any help, Chief?"

The chief motioned him inside. Ted Adams stood quietly with his hands behind his back, chest out and head held high. Eye to eye with Cyrus, he nodded a greeting, which Cyrus warily returned.

"Why don't you have a seat, Cyrus," Officer Adams suggested.

Cyrus shifted his stance. "Don't mind if I do," he sniffed, settling his large frame back in the chair he had so recently vacated. I squeezed my eyes shut tight and rubbed my forehead where the headache was starting to spread.

"Now, Ms. Palevac, Mr. Davis, what do you have here?" Chief Stoney asked.

"Let me say for the record, I don't know nothin' about nothin', especially why I have been pulled in to some sort of unsavory business," Cyrus stated with a snort.

"Listen, Chief, Cyrus took that," I pointed at the innocent looking envelope on the desk, "from my windshield because it was getting wet. He couldn't have known not to touch it, but I did, as you can see by the napkin here." I held up the bunched up napkin in my hand. "So if they're any fingerprints, they aren't mine."

"Whaddya mean fingerprints?" Cyrus leaned forward in his seat and looked over at me. The nostrils of his nose, which has been broken in three places, I might add, flared.

Chief Stoney opened his desk drawer and pulled on a pair of latex gloves. Boy, these guys have those things everywhere. He picked up the sealed envelope, opened it, and removed a folded piece of ordinary white paper. As he spread it out on his desk, Cyrus, Adams and I all angled in for a better look.

The mismatched letters read: SO MANY SURFERS SO LITTLE TIME. WHO WILL BE NEXT KELL?

"All right, you two, start talking," Chief Stoney intoned, face grim and eyes laser sharp. "You say this was on Kell's windshield, Cyrus? How did it get there?"

"The hell if I know! I was just walkin' from the Coast to grab some grub, mindin' my own business, when I saw it on Kell's windshield and it was startin' to rain fairly good, so I took it off and gave it to her when she came outside," he said. I reached over and patted his hand.

"Exactly." I said. "And here we are delivering the evidence to the authorities, exactly like we're supposed to do, except for maybe Cyrus' fingerprints and all."

"I didn't know not to touch it. How're ya gonna pick somethin' up if ya can't touch it," Cyrus mumbled.

I patted his hand again. "It's sort of confusing, Cyrus."

"All right," Chief Stoney stood up behind his desk. "Adams, get on some gloves and test this for prints, then bag it. You two, not a word of this to anyone, hear?"

Cyrus and I nodded, said our good-byes, and made our way down the hall together in hushed silence. My bare feet were cold against the hard floor. "Um, Cyrus? Thanks for getting that envelope for me, by the way."

Cyrus was becoming more and more like his old self the closer we got to the front of the building. He swaggered a bit in his boots, hands in the pockets of his jeans, the black leather jacket pushed back enough so I could see his strong chest pushing against the pot leaf on his shirt.

"Don't mention it, darlin', just get me out of this place," he said, holding the front door open for me. "Ah, fresh air."

I glanced at him. He was acting like we'd been locked up in a cell for days, for crying out loud. "Sorry about all that, business you know."

The rain had stopped and the sky was painted a fresh pale blue, hinting at the chance the sun might even shine soon. The joke around town is if you don't like the weather on Folly, just wait a little while and it will change.

"So, make it up to your ol' buddy. Come shoot some pool at the Coast tonight, it's Friday after all." Cyrus grinned.

Friday? Okay, Friday. The Coast would be hopping. I couldn't remember the last time I'd been on a Friday, but the way the week was going it sure sounded pretty good.

"You're on, pool tonight, winner drinks free," I said.

Cyrus let out a rebel yell, gave me a hug, and wandered off. I got in my car, put on my shoes, and drove the few blocks to the paper. I planned on putting in as little time as possible to get my work done, then head home and take a nap before Friday night rolled around.

CHAPTER TWENTY-ONE

Fetch me a lager, serving wench," boomed a shrill voice from somewhere in the house. I was in the bathroom, trying to impose control upon my unruly locks by spraying the mess with some goo guaranteed to coax one's curls into a luxurious mane. So far I was thinking I deserved a refund. I flipped my head forward, scrunched the strands a bit, and flipped upright once again. Okay, so now my hair took up about twice the amount of space as usual, which should at least give me some elbow room at the Coast later on.

Fred materialized in the doorway and woofed in a decidedly worried fashion, a sort of bark with a whimper at the end.

"Where's my lager?"

Fred began to pace up and down the bathroom, a few steps this way, a few that, his woofing becoming an agitated growl.

"Ignore him, fur face, he's in a cage, he can't hurt you," I explained to Fred as Blackbeard sang out his command louder. We left the bathroom together, Fred close on my heels as we made our way to the living room and the rude parrot. Sampson was perched on top of the cage, lazily reaching a furry black paw in to swipe at Blackbeard every so often who merely pecked at the intrusion and yelled louder.

"Show me your hooters."

"Sheesh, whatever happened to Polly wants a cracker and all of that other crap most parrots say," I muttered.

"Fetch me a lager, serving wench!" Fred flopped down a foot from the cage and did his best impression of mean dog, growling and showing his teeth. Sampson took a healthy swipe at the bird, who proceeded to leap around, ruffle his feathers, and continue with his demands. Assured the three of them had each other under control, I walked to the kitchen to check the message that had come in while I was napping earlier.

I hit the button and my brother's muffled voice came through from halfway across the world.

"Kell, it's Aidan. I'm in the middle of a dust storm, but Mid called and told me what's going on there so I wanted to check in with you. Listen, stay out of trouble, small sister, and I'll try to call you later. Call Dad and Mom. Love you. Ciao."

Hopefully, the call Dad and Mom hint meant he hadn't done so yet. Not that my parents would be particularly concerned to find me in the midst of a murder or two. I grabbed and ice-cold Corona from the fridge and did my lime routine, then walked back to the living room and my wall of pictures. Moments of my life captured on film, enlarged and framed. I took a sip of my beer and contemplated one of my favorites.

I was about eight, standing at the bow of a crudely dug out wooden canoe which was manned by two dark-skinned South Americans with long bamboo poles. My hair hung in ringlets and my arms were folded across my chest as I scowled at the cascading waterfall about twenty feet away. Sitting behind me was my father, beaming and waving at the photographer, who in this case was my mother, perched in a similar set up with Aidan not far from us. We were at the top of the Iguaçu Falls, which extends from Argentina in to South America.

Next to this was a shot of four Amazon Indian children, naked except for the dark markings on their face and bodies and the spears in their hands, lined up in a row with my brother and me. We were all giggling, although I remember the elder Amazonians had refused to have their picture taken, and quickly prodded us along with their very own even larger spears right after the shot was taken. The pictures continued on, various poses of me and my family in some exotic setting or another. My parents probably wouldn't blink an eye at the exciting time I was having at Folly Beach. On the other hand, you just never know, and I was ready for Friday night.

On cue, my doorbell rang. I peeked out the curtains and seeing Mid's Mustang parked outside, opened the door to let him and Siobhan inside. She was rambling on about something and marched past me to the kitchen, returning with a beer. Mid mouthed a silent hello and we both stood and listened as Siobhan continued her one-sided conversation.

"And then I said to her, fine, Alex, fine, if you aren't going to quit cropping my photos I won't take anymore." She took a long swig from her bottle. "And do you know what that helmet head said? Well, I'll tell you what she bloody said, she said I'm the editor and I'll crop what I want! Can you believe it? I have a right mind to call me da and let him have a talk with her."

Mid and I shook our heads sympathetically. I haven't heard Siobhan threaten anyone with her father in years. He is a towering red-haired giant with a mean Irish streak and the tongue to match. As he's safely miles away in Ireland, the worst Alex could expect was a phone call, although I knew Siobhan would get over it.

She was sprawled out on the couch, her well-worn cowboy boots balanced on the table in front of her. I resisted the urge to push her feet off and sat next to her. We clinked beers.

"Ready for a round of pool?" I asked.

"You betcha," she replied.

"Listen, you two, let's try to keep it under control tonight, got it? No dancing on the pool tables," Mid said sternly. Siobhan and I looked at each other with wide eyes, turning to Mid and batting our eyelashes as innocently as possible. Really, we'd only danced on the tables last Halloween, but Mid wouldn't let us forget it.

I got to ride shotgun in the Mustang with the top down, which only enhanced the volumizing effects of the curly, big-hair thing I'd achieved earlier. When we pulled up to park as close to the Coast as we could get, being a Friday and all, I noticed Siobhan's hair was similarly arranged.

"You two look a bit wild with all the hair everywhere," Mid proclaimed. His hair, although mussed a little from the breeze, was smoothly in place.

We walked the couple blocks to the Coast, Siobhan and I strutting our stuff and acting like the wild women Mid declared us to be. I had on my faded, fitted, low rise jeans, my black leather belt with the silver buckle and a plain gray t-shirt. My money was tucked in my back pocket and for once I'd left my cell phone at home. Siobhan was dressed the same as I was, except her shirt was a low-cut, clingy shade of indigo blue.

At least fifteen Harley Davidson bikes were lined up out front of the Coast, some of the owners hanging around outside talking bike lingo. I didn't see Cyrus when we walked in, so we made our way to the other side of the bar area, where the pool tables are. There's only three, so sometimes you have to get in line for a game, but tonight there was one table open. I grabbed a cue stick and laid claim while Mid edged his way to the counter for drinks.

"Good crowd tonight, and it's early yet, not even nine," Siobhan said, scanning the area. Her eyes narrowed. "Oh, goodie, our dear co-workers are here."

I grabbed a stool and straddled it, took the beer Mid handed me and set it on the ledge that runs along the wall around the pool tables. We looked at the booth closest to us where Siobhan had spotted Holly, Kenneth and Hans. Holly and Kenneth had their heads together gossiping, most likely, but Hans had seen us and stared stoney-faced in our direction. I wiggled my fingers at him and Siobhan blew him a kiss but his expression didn't change.

"He does speak English, doesn't he?" Siobhan asked, racking up the balls.

"Only when he wants to," I answered.

"I think Mid intimidates him," she declared, expertly breaking and sinking a stripe in the corner pocket.

Hans picked this moment to stand up. His face was graced with full lips beneath a straight nose and pale blue eyes, topped with hair so blond it was almost white, parted down the middle and hanging to his chin. A skin-tight white t-shirt clung to his overdeveloped torso and exposed biceps the size of grapefruits. Equally tight jeans molded themselves to legs the size of tree trunks. He strode towards the bathrooms, giving us another stoic glance on his way.

"Yeah, right," Mid mumbled, running his hand through his hair and chugging half his beer in one gulp.

"You do, sweetie, just look how rumpled his jeans are compared to yours." I patted his shoulder.

Siobhan was staring at Hans's departing figure. "What a waste of manhood," she sighed. "Nine ball, right pocket."

Lynrd Synrd was belting out "Sweet Home Alabama" on the jukebox. The live music didn't start until ten p.m. and so far nobody was dancing. I hopped off my stool, took a shot and missed. Siobhan chuckled and quickly circled the table, sinking a ball here and a ball there until only the eight ball was left.

"Eight ball, side pocket," she sang out and ended our game before I had another chance. "So, next victim?"

The four men at the table next to us were finishing up their game, too, and flipped coins to see who got to take Siobhan up on the offer. She seemed pleased with the winner, a stocky fellow with a shock of jet black hair and high cheekbones.

"I hear you called Aidan on my behalf." I wrinkled my nose at Mid. He nodded, staring intently at the bar. I followed his look, and spotted two matching women sitting side by side on stools not far from us. Long, silky bleached blond tresses hung down each back and both sported rather large, quite possibly surgically enhanced, chests.

I held my hand up and passed it in front of Mid's eyes. "Those are the Budweiser girls. Twins." He swallowed, finishing his beer. "I'm getting another, you want one?"

"Sure," I said but he was already at the bar. Sure enough, the twins caught one glimpse of Middleton and he was oohed and aahed over and given the seat of honor right smack dab in the middle of them. So much for my beer. I slid off my stool and decided to fend for myself.

Siobhan gave me a light wack on my behind with the pool stick as I passed. She was making mincemeat out of her pool partner, who was basking in the light of all the attention she was bestowing on him. I grinned at her and marched past Holly, Kenneth and Hans on my way to the restroom without even a hello. Holly was glaring at Mid's back, a stricken look on her face as the twins took turns rubbing Mid's shoulders. She downed the drink in front of her and I heard her ordering Hans to get her another gin and tonic.

The crowd was getting thicker, and I said a hello here and

there as I threaded my way through towards the back and the bathrooms. I kept an eye out for Cyrus, who probably wasn't at work yet. Directly in front of me, the line for the ladies bathroom was eight people deep so I pulled up the rear and waited my turn.

The band was warming up on the small stage. In between the guitars, drums and violin I heard the rat-a-tat-tat of machine gun laughter off to my left. Sure enough, Chelsea Chester and her band of-what had Cristina called them-posers. Unnoticed, I took a moment to observe my old school chum.

Her hair was cut in a sleek, short style that gave her a rather androgynous appearance and suited her pronounced cheek bones and sharp, clear chin. A cigarette hung between her fingers and she nervously tapped it several times in to an ashtray before putting it to her lips. Her three companions had to be a good ten years younger. As if she felt my stare, Chelsea turned her head suddenly and caught me eyes. Hers immediately looked side to side as if surprised to see me, then fixed me with a defiant look and a smirk as she blew a stream of smoke in my direction. She lifted her chin and turned back to her table of friends while I resisted the strange urge to just march over to her and say, hey, let's let bygones be bygones. Folly is a small town, and if she was living here now I certainly didn't want her as an enemy. On the other hand, there was no sense dragging up the past with someone as unstable as Chelsea had been back in college. Sure, people change, but now wasn't the time to check on Chelsea's progress, or lack thereof.

"Kell! How good to see you! Say hello to Kell, dear," ordered a perky voice interrupting my thoughts. I turned to find Mayor McLeod and Bonnie at my side, got a quick hug from each, then stood for around five minutes while Bonnie bent my ear about her latest issue on the importance of electronic fencing.

"So I told George, George we really need to make it an ordinance on Folly," Bonnie shouted above the sounds of the band, who were opening with a rendition of Van Morrison's "Brown Eyed Girl".

"And I told her there was no way in a hill of beans council would ever pass it," Mayor McLeod shouted back.

I must have missed something in the noise, so I told them both I'd be in touch. I'd missed my turn for the bathroom and the line was even longer now, so I went to the bar in search of a beer instead.

Armed with my Corona, I went back to the pool table where Siobhan was holding court. She has perfected the art of bending over just far enough to cause a commotion when it's her turn, and a couple guys bumped into each other while I watched.

"Yes! I win again! A shot of tequila for me and my mate, Brad," she ordered, throwing an arm around my shoulder. Brad with the dark hair and cheek bones trotted off like a trained horse towards the bar.

"You sure we should drink a shot? Is Mid still driving us home tonight?" I asked as Siobhan and I perched on the tall stools near the pool table. We looked towards the dance floor where several people had started to gather, Mid and the twins among them. Our favorite Southern boy was currently practicing a bit of dirty dancing with the two women, who were identically dressed in micro shorts, platform sandals and form fitting white t-shirts with the Budweiser emblem on the back.

"How do you suppose they stay so tan?" I wondered,

watching as the crowd gave the three some space. "And what's got in to Mid? He's sure letting loose tonight."

"It was the sight of twins, did him in, put him right over the edge," Siobhan answered with an air of authority. There was a sudden commotion at the booth nearby as Holly stood up and shoved Linski out of her way.

"Move it, Kenneth! Don't touch me, Hans," Holly yelled as she stumbled away from the booth, drink in hand.

Siobhan and I grabbed the shots Brad had returned with and downed them. She grabbed my arm. "Come on, this is getting good!" We followed Holly as she weaved towards the dance floor.

My not so favorite Southern belle was decked out in some sort of long yellow linen tunic dress and flat leather sandals. She watched transfixed as Mid continued to gyrate with the twins. Kenneth and Hans bumped in to us as we stood watching Holly watch Mid.

"Do something, Hans, she is completely sauced and might do something embarrassing," Kenneth whined, dragging his hand up through his spiky hair. Siobhan and I grinned at each other. Hans made a move towards Holly and we both grabbed on to his brawny biceps.

"Leave the poor dear be," Siobhan said. Hans made moves to shake us loose at the same time Holly expertly tossed her drink directly on the front of a twin. The band kept playing their Southern rock tunes as the twins stopped dancing and inspected the damage, glancing curiously at Holly who was by now screaming at Mid to behave himself. With identical shrugs, the wet t-shirt twin pulled her top off over her head and flung it to the crowd dancing around her. She and her twin boogied away from the deranged looking Holly while Mid watched them depart.

Now, you would think this would have caused a huge commotion, but, hey, this is Folly. I noticed one of the bouncers edging his way through the pack of dancers with a towel presumably to cover the twin up with, but that's about all that happened. Well, that and Holly puking on Mid's shoes and being carted off over Hans' shoulder with Kenneth in tow.

CHAPTER TWENTY-TWO

Normally I like Saturdays. Sometimes I may have to work, covering an event on Folly like an art festival or a sand-sculpting contest, which usually turns out to be an enjoyable was to spend the afternoon. This morning I was puttering around the house being domestic, doing laundry, dusting and listening to Fred and Sampson complain about their new sibling. Blackbeard was certainly living up to his namesake's reputation as a ruthless, foul-mouthed buccaneer,

"Aye, cowardly puppies, swab the deck," he screeched as I walked by with a dust rag.

"Didn't you get decapitated eventually?" I asked the parrot.

Fred growled then whimpered and Sampson hissed and showed his fangs as the two circled the cage. They were wearing a path in my carpet but Blackbeard didn't seem concerned with their attention.

"I'm horny, wanna have sex?" I looked at the can of dusting spray in my hand and considered turning it on him, but counted to ten instead. I polished my bookshelf, trying to reach all the nooks and crannies, and reflected on last night's festivities.

As Mid couldn't remain out in public with puked on shoes, we ended our evening early, which was fine by me but Siobhan insisted on one last round of pool. I used the time to check with the bartender and some of the other bouncers as to Cyrus' whereabouts, but nobody knew where he was. I was a little huffy at being stood up but otherwise didn't worry about him. The guy's a biker, for heaven's sake. The Budweiser twins, both fully dressed, were mud wrestling in the pit as we were leaving and Mid gave them one last forlorn glance as we walked away. I tried the I-told-you-so bit about Holly but the poor guy really looked devastated so I quit.

Tonight was the charity fundraiser at Mid's parents' house and I was attending as both a reporter and guest. The reporting part was because the funds raised would be used by the City of Folly Beach to offset the costs of beach renourishment, an ongoing project and the responsibility of the Army Corps of Engineers, who kept coming up short on the money part. The guest part was because I'd get to be dressed up and wander around the roughly 24,000 square foot mansion.

I spent the day puttering. My plants and animals were all watered and fed, my clothes cleaned, house picked up. I made a big bowl of popcorn and read a book, snoozed a little, gabbed with Siobhan on the phone about what to wear, then began getting ready for the evening. Freshly showered, I took extra time blow drying my hair and carefully applied more make-up than usual.

Protocol demanded a dress for the event, so I wiggled into a sleeveless, cream colored silk number, fastened my great-grandmother's pearls around my neck and squeezed my feet into three-inch beige pumps. After one final check in the mirror, I deemed myself presentable enough for society.

Standing next to Siobhan an hour later with a glass of champagne in my hand I decided that although I may be presentable, upper crust fashionable I was not.

"Bollocks, would you look at that," my friend sputtered as she sipped her champagne. Amongst the ornately coiffed and perfumed guests, Holly Chesnut was making an entrance, all signs of last night's slumming at the Coast behind her. She floated in wearing a deep-pink silk crepe garment with a chiffon skirt, her hair piled on her head with demure auburn ringlets escaping here and there. She marched right up to Mid and took hold of his arm possessively, her bright smile defying any other female to do the same.

At that moment Middleton's mother appeared and whispered something in her son's ear, then spotted me and Siobhan and held out her hands.

"Why, girls, let me hug your necks! It's been too long, y'all get on over here this skinny minute," trilled Ella Kay Heyward Calhoun, sparkling in a strapless fuchsia dress so heavily encrusted with rhinestones it probably could have stood alone. Her brown eyes, so like Mid's, flashed as she watched Holly flirt with her son.

"Whatever are we going to do about her," murmured Ella Kay. "I declare, she is just sweeter than sugar cubes in syrup."

Siobhan finished off her glass of champagne and set it on the tray of a server passing by. "Miss Holly? I thought she was something of an aristocrat around these parts."

Ella Kay snorted in the delicate way only the very wealthy can do. "Livin' in a garage don't make you a Ford." I looked at Siobhan and she shrugged her shoulders, smiling. Ella Kay is a descendent of the original Heywards, and a relative of Dubose Heyward of Porgy and Bess fame. She's also mighty feisty and bright. We made small talk about my parents, and then I left her and Siobhan alone while I wandered the mansion. All of the rooms on the main floor were open and flowing with a variety of hors d'oeuvres and beverages. The rooms are all opulently decorated with individual color schemes and referred to as the green room, the yellow room and so forth. I discreetly removed my little notebook from my evening bag and took notes, penning in who was here and what they were wearing.

I retreated to a corner of the room I was in, the blue room, and took a seat in a midnight-blue chair, rereading my scribbles. All of town council was here, along with many of Folly's residents. I even spotted Ludmilla and Murphy. The party was so crowded it was difficult to mingle with everyone, which was fine by me. Lost in thought, head bent over my notebook, I wrinkled my nose at the sudden foul smell.

"I hear you've taken to finding dead women," slurred Preston Brooks, his breath hot against my cheek. "Better watch your step."

I shrunk back. "Go brush your teeth."

Judge Brooks straightened up, his face contorting into a purplish mask of fury. "Someone needs to teach you some manners, girl," he sneered, slinking away.

I resisted the urge to kick off my heels and tuck my feet under the chair. He always made me feel there were rats lurking around. On cue, Chelsea Chester entered the room dressed in a black silky pantsuit. Of course she would be here, I'd heard she was one of the most generous donors. Since her return to town, I'd found out about the death of her parents in a car crash a year earlier, hence the huge inheritance. I studied her from my corner, watching as she awkwardly lit a cigarette and avoided my gaze. I knew she'd seen me. I stood up and flounced out of the room to the best of my ability. No sense suffering in the same room as Chelsea if I didn't have to.

The evening wore on. I chatted with people, wandered the colored rooms, drank more champagne. I was just thinking of making my exit when my cell phone rang from within my small evening bag.

"Kell here," I answered.

"Upstairs, hurry, need help," a muffled voice gasped. "It's Siobhan."

"Siobhan? I can hardly understand you. Where are you?"

"Upstairs, bathroom, hurry."

I looked around. The main stairwell was too far away, so I ran as fast as my heels would let me to the back staircase down the hall. Climbing the marble steps, I tried to remember where the bathrooms were up here. The doors were all closed, except for one a little ways down the hall where a dim light crept out.

"Siobhan? Are you okay?" I called out as I hurried towards the open door. Yes! A bathroom. "Siobhan," I tried again, pushing the door open wider and surveying the area. In the muted light I saw someone sitting on a small stool beside the sink about fifteen feet in front of me. Focusing, I noticed the long blond hair and the big smile.

"Oh, sorry, I was looking for my friend," I said. The stranger just kept grinning.

"Listen, have you seen anyone else in here? Tall, red hair, green eyes?" I looked around the rest of the sizeable bathroom. "Hey, did you hear me?"

I advanced the rest of the way in, looking for somewhere Siobhan could be hiding. "Hey," I said to the stranger again, shaking her shoulder. She slid off the stool and down to the floor with a thump, her head thrown back so I could nicely inspect the smile that wasn't a smile but a bloody red gash extending from ear to ear.

CHAPTER TWENTY-THREE

Late the next day I was hobbling up to my front door, still dressed in my fancy attire of the previous evening. All I wanted was a hot shower, pajamas and my bed. Fred came outside, lifted a leg on the bushes, and returned to the house. I locked the door and poured a glass of milk, undressed, hit the shower and crawled into bed. I now knew what it felt like to be put through the ringer.

I'd handled my grim discovery slightly better than my first dead body. Okay, so I threw up, but not until I was finished screaming and sliding down the marble staircase on my rear end. Middleton, good crime reporter that he is, called the police and secured the mansion, meaning nobody was allowed to leave. The victim was quickly identified as twenty-year-old Jessica Clayton by her horrified and distraught boyfriend who hadn't seen her for about thirty minutes. Pretty, blond-haired Jessica was deeply tanned from her recent surfing trip to Costa Rica.

Many of the guests had already left the party before the murder, but the ones remaining were grilled by a swarm of Charleston police officers. It was some surreal reincarnation of the game Clue, with voices claiming to have been in the red room or the green room all evening. Nobody mentioned a candlestick, but it didn't take a reporter to figure out the murderer used a knife.

They took my cell phone and traced the incoming number to a telephone inside the mansion. I'd spent most of the evening with several of the other guests giving statements down at Charleston police headquarters, where they aren't nearly as friendly as the folks at Folly. Chief Stoney appeared, and spent some time catching up the other policemen on what had been taking place in his jurisdiction. This interesting connection to me resulted in lots more questioning by policemen and I was actually relieved the chief was there to back me up. Now that the killer had struck in Charleston County, my fame was spreading.

Exhausted, I fell into a fitful sleep before the sun went down, thankfully much too tired to let the director of my dreams have his way. I awoke Monday morning with fragments of dream-like memories, but none that I really remembered. Exercise deprived, I was feeling itchy to do something, but didn't dare venture out. I got dressed for work, grabbed my umbrella because it was starting to rain and walked around the backyard with Fred when my cell phone rang.

I looked at the numbers displayed before answering this time. Middleton.

"Kell here."

"Where exactly?"

"In my backyard."

"Come around front, I'll be pulling up in a minute."

He hung up before I could ask any questions. Fred and I went back inside, and I collected my black bag and an apple and locked my door behind me just as Mid's convertible pulled up, top raised due to the threat of rain. He was in the driver's seat with Siobhan riding shotgun. She tossed me a brown paper bag as I approached.

"Picked you up a bagel with raspberry cream cheese from Mazo's, hop in," she said.

Yummy. I climbed in the backseat and started eating. "Where're we going?" I asked with my mouth full.

Mid looked at me in his rear view mirror. "Watch the crumbs. I have to go talk to the guys at the Coast Guard Station, they're going to patrol the beach extra closely with helicopters and Alex wants the angle for your next article. We're going to share a byline."

I munched happily as we rode to Coast Guard central near the City Marina in downtown Charleston. We made our presence known, and were escorted to a room full of helicopter pilots being debriefed by the pilot in charge. We took seats at the back of the room.

Mid jotted notes while the men discussed the schedule for the upcoming week. When they got around to discussing the murders at Folly, most of the guys had started to squirm in their seats, looking at their watches and making motions to leave. Siobhan and I glanced at each other, shaking our heads. Poor Mid. These guys were done with the meeting and ready to jump back into their bright orange choppers.

"Excuse me," said Mid, holding up his pencil. "I'm from *The Archipelago* and have a quick question." Some of the pilots were pulling on jackets by now.

"Um, sure," said the pilot in charge from the front of the room.

Mid cleared his throat. "Well, the folks at Folly are sure appreciative of the extra work you guys will be putting in over there, and some of the surfer girls mentioned they were planning to start flashing the chopper as it went by."

These Coast Guard guys must get hired for their hearing as four or five of them leaned over at once and said, "What?"

"Yes, well, you guys get people waving and kids saluting you and all that, and the girls just wanted to say thank-you in more of a Folly Beach fashion," Mid continued.

One of the pilots turned around in his seat. "You mean, lifting their tops kinda flashing?"

There was a collective rustle as the men about-faced it and regarded the three of us. Siobhan wiggled her fingers at them, grinning, while I slunk down in my seat. Mid certainly knew how to capture an audience.

"Well, yes, what do you guys think? I was a bit concerned one of you would call it in and get some of the girls ticketed," he said.

The room responded as one. "Not a problem."

Mid had no trouble receiving answers to a few more serious questions about the helicopter schedule for Folly, while Siobhan threw out a wave here and a smile there. I felt like a room full of lecherous chopper pilots was ogling me. My cell phone rang. I rummaged around in my bag and managed to answer before it switched to my greeting.

"Kell here."

"Um, Kell, this is Elbie."

"Hey, Elbie, what's up?" I asked, getting to my feet. The meeting was over and we were on our way out. Strange, I thought. I knew Ludmilla had my cell phone number on her refrigerator in case of emergencies, but I couldn't remember Elbie ever calling me before.

"Um, well, I wasn't spying on you, really I wasn't, I was just lonely 'cause my mom made me stay home from school today to like, settle down from the other day 'cause I'm still not feeling so great," Elbie rambled. "I was just looking down to see if you were there."

I shoved my bag up on my shoulder and walked with Mid towards the exit. Siobhan was chatting merrily with a group of pilots somewhere behind us.

"Okay, Elbie, I believe you, you weren't spying on me."

I heard a hiccup. "There's, like, someone to see you, Kell."

"At my front door? Don't pay attention, Elbie, it's probably the FedEx guy or something." Finally, a care package from my mom. "He'll just leave it on the front porch."

Hiccup. "Not at the front door. She's on your back porch. I was just looking down to see if you were there, I swear."

I froze. Mid and I were at the front of the Coast Guard Station and he was holding the door open for me. The rain hummed against the roof overhead and a burst of lighting cracked the skies apart as I looked out. Something terrifying gripped my stomach as I asked, "Who's on my back porch?"

"Another sleeping girl, Kell," Elbie said.

CHAPTER TWENTY-FOUR

I don't think Middleton Langdon Calhoun had ever broken the speed limit in his life, but as we careened up Center Street and made a hard left on to Ashley Avenue, I was sure a lunatic was at the wheel and this was a getaway car. After giving Elbie careful instructions to stay upstairs, I'd called Chief Stoney immediately.

A man walking a miniature black poodle dove in the bushes as we flew by. My heart was pounding as I glanced back in time to see him crawling out on his knees, shaking his fist at us.

In no time we were pulling up to my house, squeezing in behind two patrol cars and an unmarked vehicle. Both Ludmilla's and Murphy's cars were gone. Poor Elbie wasn't kidding when he said he was alone. The three of us jumped out and ran to the backyard.

The gate to my privacy fence was open, and we pulled up short, hesitant now. Mid led the way, and I could hear the low voices of the others who'd arrived before us. I peaked inside my gate, where Chief Stoney, Detective Alston, Officer Jacoby and another man were gathered.

"Would you do the honors, Ms. Mulvaney?" the Chief asked grimly, gesturing to the floor. Siobhan promptly unsnapped her camera bag, pulled out her Nikon and began capturing images of the figure on the ground.

The blond on the surfboard was on her back, an expression of shocked anger forever etched on her slack features. I recognized the white boat rope that trapped her to the board. She was young, pretty even in death, and wore the familiar purple rash guard. Someone had thoughtfully covered her from the waist down with one of my beach towels I'd left drying on the porch.

No one spoke. Siobhan's camera whirred as she snapped away, and the occasional seagull cried overhead. The new guy was on his knees, wearing thin latex gloves. He lifted the dead girls' hands one at a time, checking her fingernails. He picked up a small metal tool and scraped under each nail carefully, depositing his findings in a Ziploc baggie.

"This is Detective Matthew Lord, he's with the forensics unit downtown." Chief Stoney's voice was raspy and flat, his shoulders slumped forward and an air of defeat imprinted on his face. I knew how he felt.

Detective Alston walked out of the gate and into the backyard. The rest of us followed, leaving Siobhan and Detective Lord to their work. Alston's gaze was fixed on the creek behind my house, and he headed in that direction, the rest of us trailing behind silently. He paused when he reached a small pile of ashes, pieces of plastic visible here and there, and nudged it with the tip of his loafer.

"That's nothing, just Elbie," I said.

We continued on until we were at the edge of the property, pluff mud and marsh grass hiding piles of oyster beds. The tide was high in the creek, the water about a foot lower than the land. The rainy morning had softened the earth and there was a slight indentation about a foot wide over on the edge of the yard.

Detective Alston walked over, knelt down, and ran his hand over the matted down grass. "Right here," he said, motioning to the chief. We gathered around.

I was bursting with questions and the bagel I'd inhaled earlier, but I swallowed hard, keeping everything down. Mid's face was somber, and Jacoby was pinching the bridge of his nose. Out of the blue, a great heron suddenly flapped its wings, taking flight from its hiding spot in the creek.

"Someone approached in the creek, probably in a skiff or a runabout, and pushed the board up right here." Detective Alston indicated the creek's edge. "Then they drug it through the yard over there, alongside the fence, and then in to your porch area, Ms. Palevac."

I looked up from the grass to see him eyeing me questioningly. Come to think of it, so was the chief, and Jacoby, too.

"What, do you think I invited her over for tea and cookies?" I retorted. "Don't start with me, I don't feel so great."

Mid changed the subject by asking, "Is that how the last girl got on the beach, too?"

Detective Alston answered, "Yes, we believe someone approached the east end of the island in a small boat, waiting until Ms. Palevac had disappeared around the bend, and pulled the board up on shore. There were similar marks in the sand."

Siobhan and Detective Lord materialized from my porch, and we walked towards them just as the sounds of doors slamming resounded in the eerily silent day. The emergency medical team had arrived to transport the body on to the coroner's office, although I already knew she had been strangled to death. I'd seen the marks on her neck.

A pounding on an upstairs window captured everyone's attention. Elbie had his nose pressed flat against the pane of glass.

"Ah, yes, Elbert Dubrov. Let's get him in a squad car and bring him to the station to issue a statement," Chief Stoney instructed Officer Jacoby.

"But he's a minor," I protested.

"So I'll call his mother," the chief barked.

Overruled, I went off to collect Elbie with Siobhan in tow. He was babbling so incoherently I knew his statement would be useless.

"Come on, Elbie, let's ride down to the police station," I said, nudging him along.

He was shaking and hiccupping, and the two of us had to hold him up by both arms.

"Sheesh, he's heavy, and absolutely delirious. They might have to sedate him down at headquarters," Siobhan panted.

"He's not the only one," I muttered, steering Elbie towards the waiting squad car.

CHAPTER TWENTY-FIVE

The station became a hub of noise and confusion as Elbie, Siobhan, Mid and I joined the chief and Detective Alston in a conference room. Connie Albright, ready for all incoming calls, gaped at us, eyes like saucers and surprisingly silent as we trekked on by.

Once seated, Chief Stoney turned to Siobhan. "May I have the roll of film you took of the victim, Ms. Mulvaney?" he asked with an outstretched hand.

"What? That film belongs to the paper." Siobhan clasped her camera bag to her chest.

"We'll reimburse them," Chief Stoney drawled.

Siobhan reluctantly rewound the film and tossed it to the chief. I shook my head. No way was Mr.Lyons running those shots, anyway.

Mid and Detective Alston were both sitting with hands clasped in front of them on the table, Elbie picked at a scab on his arm until it bled, and I fidgeted in my chair. Chief Stoney began asking us all questions, taking notes on the yellow legal pad in front of him. When he finished, he pushed his chair back and looked around the room. Detective Alston spoke up.

"Now, what we have to go on at this point is a bizarre connection between the murders and Ms. Palevac," he began, his gray eyes flat and expressionless.

"The victim from Saturday evening was clearly killed in a different manner, a violent act of rage. There was no time for a slower method like strangulation."

"So does this mean it was a different killer, perhaps?" Mid asked.

"Possible, but the phone call to Kell prompting her to the scene of the crime indicates the same need to shock or warn her in some way," Detective Alston replied. He turned in his chair and fixed me with his obscure obsidian gaze. "I'd like you to make a list of anyone you may have offended in your reporting."

Siobhan made a noise somewhere between a laugh and a grunt and Mid shook his head, staring at the table. Detective Alston raised his eyebrows.

"Kell writes about human interest events, stuff like that......" Siobhan began.

Mid was talking at the same time. ".........you know, Detective, we even call it the fluffy stuff. She never writes a derogatory comment about anyone."

"For the love of God, she's the reporter for a beach town," Siobhan continued with just a bit too much sarcasm for my liking. I looked back and forth at them, wondering how often they discussed my career.

"Well, Judge Brooks is never too happy when I report on him losing his zoning appeal," I retorted, crossing my arms over my chest. The detective glanced at the chief, who scribbled in his notepad.

I searched my memory. "How about Lurleen Higgenbottom? She was pretty upset about the article I did on her ceramics class."

"That's because you spelled her name wrong," Siobhan reminded me.

Detective Alston massaged his forehead and interrupted. "Okay, well, you've got the idea."

My cell phone rang.

"Sorry," I said, answering quickly. "Kell here."

"Kell? This is Murph," he slurred.

"Murphy? Where are you?" The chief motioned me to take my call out to the hallway. I left, closing the door behind me.

"Shright here, shilly," Murphy sniggered.

"Okay, Murphy, what's going on?" I paced a few feet down the hallway.

Murphy belched so loudly I could have sworn he was right around the corner. I walked further down the hallway and poked my head about. Sure enough, there he was at the pay phone they must use to let inmates make their one allotted call. Huh, I'd never seen it before.

I hung up my phone and walked towards Murphy. "Kell, don't hang up, please," he pleaded, whining like a baby. I tapped him on the shoulder.

"Aaargh," he shouted. Officer McClellan shot to his feet from the chair he was dozing in, took one look at me and shouted, "Aaargh," too. I sure was having a funny effect on people around here.

"You again," he growled.

"My angel," Murphy blubbered, falling in to my arms.

He stank of alcohol and was sticky and sweaty, dark hair falling loose around his deeply tanned face. I pushed him off me.

"Okay, Yankee, back in the cell," McClellan pulled Murphy and led him unsteadily away.

"Wait, Kell, come here," Murphy cried, suddenly lucid. "Give her my keys!"

McClellan slammed the cell door shut, locking it resoundingly.

He huffed a little, pulling his pants up further so they nestled under his protruding belly. Reaching in his pocket, he tossed me a set of keys on a silver mermaid key chain.

"To my boat, someone needs to turn the bilge pump on," Murphy slurred. "Can't find Ludmilla."

"Probably because she's on her way here to help Elbie," I stated.

"Elbie's here, too? Told her she should take that exacto knife away from that kid." Murphy's head found the cot in his new room.

I turned to McClellan. "What's he doing in here?"

"Darn fool was at the Coast, running his fool mouth to some biker boys," McClellan said. "Ranting on about how the North won the war, and how uneducated us Southern boys are. Couple fellows were just starting to whistle Dixie on his head when someone called us." He jerked his thumb in Murphy's direction. "Lucky for him."

I winced. Murphy had better start paying attention to those bumper stickers that say I don't care how you do it up north. People don't play in this town. At least Murphy was safely locked up, at least for the day, which gave me one less person to wonder about. Paranoia was setting in and I'd become suspicious of everybody.

A familiar laugh echoed off the walls of the police station.

"Officer McClellan, what's she doing here?" I asked, motioning towards the genderless figure.

"Who, her? She's the resident badge bunny," McClellan chuckled.

The short, dark hair swung as the short, compact outline shook with hilarity. There it was again, the earsplitting sound of her laugh.

"Badge bunny?"

"Yeah, you know, someone who'll date anyone with a badge, that's what we call 'em. Chelsea actually wanted to be a cop, couldn't pass the test, so we let her hang around here," he said. He leaned forward. "She's loaded, too. Parents died last year and left her a fortune. Some folks say they were killed."

"Hmm, you don't say." I continued to stare down the hall at the girl surrounded by police officers. "Killed how?"

Officer McClellan took a dingy handkerchief out of his pocket and wiped the sweat off his brow. "Someone tampered with the brakes on their car, they went straight off a cliff. I reckon the poor girl needs friends, so she comes by now and again."

Chelsea Chester, resident badge bunny, abruptly stopped laughing and glanced my way. Her eyes did a long, slow slide over me, coming up until they met mine. From the distance I couldn't see their color, but I sensed the defiance radiating out towards me. My tension rose a few more percentage points as she graced me with a smirking wink and turned her back. I shuddered.

"Um, thanks for the keys," I told McClellan.

He waved me away. "About time he reached someone, kept hollering for somebody to get to his boat."

I glanced over at the snoring shape of Murphy. "I'll send his girlfriend for him later."

I walked slowly back towards the conference room, trying to sort out my thoughts, arrange them and impose order, but it was no use. I had another dead girl to deal with, this one a bit too close to home for my liking, and the rat-a-tat-tat of laughter kept echoing in my head.

I sighed. Time to head to the Maritime Marina to turn on Murphy's bilge pump, whatever that was.

CHAPTER TWENTY-SIX

The door to the conference room opened just as I was attempting to slip away unnoticed. I was tired of discussing these dead girls and the implication that this was in some bizarre way connected to me. Me? The idea was so utterly absurd I was simply going to go about my business as normal. Go to the marina for Murphy, then head to the newspaper and answer the slew of messages most likely piling up. Pester Holly a bit, banter with Linski and then maybe give Bonnie a call. She really had been quite patient during the events of the last few days, and I needed to catch up on the whole Exotic Animal Ordinance thing. Okay, so maybe I was more like Scarlett O'Hara than I thought, choosing to think about the bad stuff later. Maybe it was just denial. Either way, I was reaching my limit.

I bumped into Ludmilla and Elbie as they came out of the room. Elbie's eyes were glazed over and his mother had her arm around his shoulder.

"Hello, Kell, I just got here and I'm taking Elbert to work with me for the day. He desperately needs an adjustment and I don't want him alone at the house under the circumstances." Ludmilla frowned at me.

"I can understand that, Ludmilla," I said, wanting to scream this is not my fault! I swallowed. "Murphy's in the cell around the corner, by the way."

She didn't miss a beat, just kept walking away with Elbie in tow. "A good place for him," she pronounced.

Elbie looked back over his shoulder and gave me a wide grin. "Hey, your police friends locked him up after all!"

I waved good-bye. The room emptied in to the hallway, and I was surrounded. So much for slipping away, I sighed.

"Kell, there you are," said Mid. "Listen, let's head to the paper and go over this with Alex, she's probably chomping at the bit by now."

"I'll meet you guys there, I've got an errand to run first."

"Take Siobhan with you, then, you don't need to be running around alone out there," Mid said, slipping his sunglasses in place as he left.

Oh, for heaven's sake, he made it sound like I'd be gallivanting around a major city unattended. This was Folly Beach, my home, and I was a bit fed up with all the drama. I made a face at Siobhan, which she returned.

"He is right, Ms. Palevac, and Chief Stoney is assigning an officer to your house this evening for your protection," Detective Alston said. Well, at least they'd determined which side I was on.

Connie was on the phone talking in muted whispers as we left. Siobhan gave her a grin and I waved, but Connie just kept talking, glancing at us furtively from beneath hooded eyelids.

"Blimey, she must think we have something catchy," Siobhan mused. "Where to, darlin'?"

We walked the length of the building towards the front doors, our footsteps reverberating on the marbled floors. Outside the drizzle of earlier had given way to a cushioning silence of fog as we left the building, completing the ill at ease mood settling over the day.

"I've got to go to the Maritime Marina to check on Murphy's boat, something about the bilge pump. You mind walking? It's just past the paper, you know, back behind those apartments," I said.

We walked together in a companionable silence for a while, acknowledging beeps here and there from passing cars and people on bikes. I prayed the officials would catch whoever was up to all this nonsense. I wanted to feel normal again.

"I had another dream the other night," I told Siobhan, switching my heavy black bag from one shoulder to the other.

Siobhan did the same with her camera bag. "Do tell," she said.

"Well, it was sort of like the first one," I said, not mentioning the various forms of sea life in my second dream. "They said, the answers are in the water, something like that."

"Hmmm. Maybe we should go surfing again," Siobhan said as we turned on to the path leading to the marina.

"Maybe," I agreed.

We approached the marina, watching the pelicans resting on top of the small store at the end of one of the long docks. I heard the sharp, brittle crack of weathered wood as we stepped up on the first dock, and looked down. The water rippled underneath where I saw it between the planks.

"Sounds like they need new docks," Siobhan muttered, gathering up her hair and securing it with a barrette. I looked closer. My barrette, actually.

My own unruly mane had a life of its own, thrashing around in the wind as if ready to lift me skyward. I shoved it behind my ears.

"Okay, there's Murphy's boat in that slip over there." I pointed to the dock two over from where we stood. "I'm going to get this over with so we can get back to work."

"Need any help? If not, I'm going to walk down towards the marina store and take some pictures of the pelicans," Siobhan said.

I waved her on. "I can handle this. Meet you back here in a few."

I inhaled the smell of low tide and crawling things and admired a beautiful, snow-white egret take flight from its perch on the dock as I passed. There was a splashing sound in the water, and I looked over just in time to see two dolphins rising playfully up, backs arched as they went under again. All the wondrous creatures of the low country were saying hello today, and the thought cheered me. Walking out on the dock, I was surrounded by water and the sounds of boats groaning at their ropes, bumping in to the dock now and then, anxious to head out to sea once more.

"You'll find the answers in the water, Kell," Darla's voice promised from my dream.

"Will you shut up," I said. "I have to figure out how to turn Murphy's bilge pump on."

I reached Murphy's fishing trawler, aptly named *Life of the Party,* and climbed aboard. I set my bag down and looked around. The door to the cabin was ajar, so I walked over and took a quick peek inside. Murphy had taken a few of us out for a ride one evening a few months ago, and the interior was as beautiful as I remembered, everything fancy mahogany woodwork. No bilge pump in here.

I looked up the stairs towards the pilot's house. I had no clue where to look for the mysterious bilge pump, but this seemed like a good place to start. I climbed the steps and contemplated the instrument panel.

"Can I help you with anything," came a soft, breathy voice. "I know the owner of this boat."

I jumped up and banged my head on the boat's windshield. Down on the dock was a young woman with long, silky blond hair, a College of Charleston baseball cap pulled down on her head and dark sunglasses perched on her nose.

I laughed. "You startled me. Um, sure, well, do you know how to turn the bilge pump on?" She looked vaguely familiar and I eyed her curiously.

She climbed aboard, comfortable in the boat in a way I wasn't, and walked up the stairs. She flicked a green switch on the instrument panel and something hummed to life. "Bilge pump," she smiled.

"Thanks," I told her, relieved my mission was accomplished. "I owe you one. What did you say your name was?"

"I didn't," said the blond, reaching behind her back. "But I know your name, Kell. And you're right, you do owe me one. In fact, you've owed me one for a long, long time now."

I felt the jab of something in my back. "Just start walking, I'll point you in the right direction."

I made a move to jerk away. "This is a .38 caliber complete with a silencer, so if you'd like we can get this over with right here," she said with amusement.

I contemplated my options. Yell for help and get shot on the spot, or take my chances with blondie here. I now knew what it felt like to walk the plank, my feet like lead as I walked down the steps, the gun nudging me along.

CHAPTER TWENTY-SEVEN

The dock creaked under my feet as we moved quickly in the opposite direction of the marina store, the gun prodding me along. Out of the corner of my eye I spotted Siobhan merrily snapping away with her back to me, oblivious to my mortal dilemma. I truly wanted to scream, or at least bawl like a baby, but blondie kept jabbing me with the firearm.

"Keep moving. See that man up ahead fishing? That's Jake. Don't open your mouth, just keep walking past him."

Oh, joy, at least someone would see me. Whatever was going on here, I didn't like it, and a witness was bound to come in handy. I fixated on the elderly black fellow sitting on an overturned paint can, fishing pole in hand. He raised his head, cocking it as we approached.

Filmy, unseeing eyes glazed blankly to our left. My only witness was blind. Blondie nudged me on.

"It's just me, Jake. Catching much?" she asked.

Jake's voice rumbled deep and raspy in his chest. "Not yet, missy, but I got all day. Goin' out in your boat?"

"Yes, as a matter of fact, she needs to run some," Blondie replied. Wonderful, I hope she didn't think I was going along for the excursion.

We passed several boats secure in their slips and kept going, all the way to the last dock. We stopped at the end where a beautiful cabin cruiser bobbed in the water, *Emotional Rescue* painted on the stern in gilded lettering.

Blondie looked around. "Climb aboard," she hissed. I obeyed.

She followed, shoving me ahead of her. She opened the door to the cabin and pushed me through, closed the door and locked it from the outside.

I landed on my hands and knees and hastily scrambled to my feet. I surveyed my surroundings. I was in a rather lovely galley area, with a stove, sink and refrigerator to my left, a bathroom to my right and a dinette set straight ahead encircled by a burgundy-colored couch. Blondie wasn't much of a housekeeper. The place looked like a bombed-out haberdashery, with clothing and small items of gear strewn about haphazardly.

Sick to my stomach with dread, I maneuvered around a large cooler occupying most of the walk area and sat gingerly on a corner of the couch. As the engine roared to life I studied the walls around me with complete disbelief.

I was everywhere. Hundreds of pictures were taped up, overlapping in places, but all of me. Me jogging on the beach. Me laughing. Me walking hand and hand with Fletcher. I was on my knees, frantically flipping through the photographs. Me walking around campus. Most of these shots were at least five years old. I inhaled deeply, holding my breath until the count of ten and blowing it out. Again. I could not hyperventilate. What in the world was happening?

The engine was idling as the door opened suddenly. My kidnapper pulled her hat and sunglasses off, then reached up and yanked at the long blond wig, tossing them in my direction. She kept the gun in her hand pointed at me.

I gasped. The badge bunny. Chelsea Chester.

"You didn't recognize me, did you, Kell? But then again, you barely even knew I existed. Like my pictures, Kell?" She slid in next to me. I shrank back when she reached out to touch my hair. "I always wished I had your hair."

I gulped. "You can have it, let's just chop it right off and be done with this and I'll be on my way."

Her pale blue eyes darted wildly around the cabin, the gun in her hand jerking. I flinched.

"Oh, no, you can't leave, Kell, you just got here." Her short brown hair was beginning to stick to her forehead with sweat. She looked at the watch on her arm. "We have to shove off, out to sea we go before any of your nosey friends come poking around." Chelsea Chester fixed me with her eyes, the pupils dilated. "I would have been your friend, but you ignored me," she said, standing up.

Maybe if I kept her talking Siobhan would quit taking pictures long enough to come to my rescue. "What are you talking about? I didn't ignore you, we just didn't have any classes together."

Whoops, wrong answer. Chelsea unsheathed a large knife from her side, switched the gun to her other hand and held the tip of the knife to my neck. I winced as the cold blade pressed my skin, Chelsea's face a mixture of crazed emotions inches from mine.

"You snubbed me! Me! You and your friends, but especially you, Kell. Do you know how humiliated I was? You and that red-haired Irish princess, such good friends," she wheezed, her breath coming in short bursts. "I tried to get her out of the way, Fletcher, too." I felt a sharp sting and a warm trickle as the knife pressed harder into my neck.

I closed my eyes. "I'm sorry if I hurt you in any way, Chelsea," I whispered. "I didn't understand."

The pressure on my neck was removed. "It's probably for the best I wasn't successful removing those two. You see, I didn't understand then either. But I finally do. You're the one, Kell."

She closed the cabin door behind her as she left, locking it, and within minutes we were pulling away from the dock. I watched through the portholes as the marina became smaller and smaller as we set out for parts unknown.

CHAPTER TWENTY-EIGHT

The engine droned on as the cruiser raced through the water. I attempted to keep my bearings by continuing to watch through the portholes, but my insides were cramping up and nausea was overwhelming me. I staggered to the bathroom, opened the door, and threw up. I was heaving, holding my hair back from my face when I spotted the purple rash guard hanging on a hook.

My body went rigid and I heard the roar of blood in my ears as I comprehended the severity of my situation. Chelsea Chester was the killer. No more Scarlett denial time. My heart was hammering so loudly in my chest I was sure she could hear it.

I went to the sink, ran the water and rinsed out my mouth. I spat, turned the water off and tried to slow down the freight train in my head. I was out in the ocean with a killer. I was dead. This was it. I'd never see Fred or Sampson again. My breath came in short staccato bursts and I began ro hyperventilate. Creeping towards the sofa, I sat back down and hung my head between my legs. The engine stopped, and I heard the sound of something splashing overboard. Chelsea? Hopefully, I scrambled to my knees, peering out a porthole. I couldn't see anything. I went to the other side, and could make out the Holiday Inn far off in the distance. At least we weren't too far from land.

The door to the cabin flew open and I shrieked. "You know, Chelsea, I was thinking here while you were driving. I do remember having a class with you," I lied, my heart pounding in my ears.

She narrowed her eyes warily at me, reaching in the refrigerator and pulling out two Coronas and a lime, which she sliced in wedges with her pointy knife. Flipping the tops off the beers, she placed one lime in her bottle and two in mine, handing it to me. Oh, goody, happy hour.

I cleared my throat. "Corona, my favorite."

"I know," she said.

I raised my bottle in a toast. "Cheers."

She tilted her head back, finishing half her beer in one swallow. I took a sip of mine and held back the gag in my throat.

"We were in economics together my junior year. You were a senior," Chelsea said, wiping her mouth with the back of her hand.

My brain raced. Economics. Senior year. McDuffie's class. Right. I'd failed and had to retake it before I could graduate.

"Mr. McDuffie's class," I blurted out.

Chelsea's eyes brightened. "You do remember," she smiled, her sharp cheek bones rising. "I was always trying to get your attention, but you were always with Fletcher." She spat the name out, her face clouding over. "I'm a much better surfer than he ever was, you should have let me teach you."

My mind spun back to my college days at the beach. Did I remember her? Vaguely, maybe a figure on the outskirts of my days, paddling by, perhaps, as I sat laughing in the water with Fletcher. I couldn't be sure.

Chelsea finished her beer, retrieved another, and sat down on the couch. Her eyes were hazy, glazed over by more than the beer. She looked at the pictures on the wall.

"You hardly ever spoke to me," she began, her voice low and dreamy. "You were so popular, so smart and beautiful." I looked around the cabin. Me? She was talking to me? "And out in the water, you'd sit on your board and joke around with everyone, and I wanted to be you." Her voice had taken on a breathy, little girl's tone.

I gulped my beer, the liquid hitting my empty stomach like fire. Chelsea continued her dialogue.

"I kept track of you after you graduated. You became this famous reporter, and soon you were hanging out with policemen, so I decided to become a cop, but even that didn't work." She slammed her beer bottle down on the table. I winced.

"So what did you do after college?" I asked, spotting the knife safely back at her side. She waved the gun around carelessly and I shrunk back.

"I moved back home and lived with my parents, of course," Chelsea sneered. "Father was so busy traveling all the time and Mother was so lonely, poor dear. I'm an only child. Figure I'd wait until they both kicked it, get my inheritance and be free, but they weren't showing signs of going anywhere."

She leaned forward, so close to me I could see the vein pulsing in her forehead. "Guess what I did? Sliced the wires on Father's Mercedes so the breaks failed when they went out one night. It worked.." She burst out laughing. "And I got all the money. I moved back here, but you still didn't notice me even after all these years."

Well, I had to give her that one.

"Once when I was out surfing I saw this girl who looked so much like you and I waited until she got out of the water. Asked her if she wanted to smoke a joint, we talked for a while, she said sure. I put our boards in my car and drove to the marina," Chelsea said. "Oh, yeah, she was nice at first, liked the boat, smoked my weed and drank my beers, but she didn't want to stay, not really." Her voice was escalating, her mouth lifting in a menacing, sarcastic smile.

She whipped her head in my direction, her icy-blue eyes radiating hatred and torment. "She was rude, Kell. Laughed at me. Not like you." I nodded my head vigorously in agreement.

She stood up abruptly, reached for another beer, and fixed one for me. "Know what I did?" she asked, her face close to mine.

I was afraid to ask. "What?"

"I choked her. Choked her so hard she quit breathing, and you know, it felt so good. Choked all the mean, ugly laughs right out of her head. But I didn't know what to do with her, so I stuck her in there with a bunch of ice." She gestured at the cooler on the floor. I pulled my feet up.

"I stayed out in the water for days, I even pulled her out of the ice and brought her above, but she kept sliding around the deck." Bile rose in the back of my throat.

"She made me so mad I nailed her hands to the floor to keep her from slipping around, but that made a mess of the deck, so I went kind of nuts and whipped her with some rope," Chelsea said almost apologetically. I jumped up, ran to the bathroom and puked.

"Sorry," I gasped, returning to the couch. "Must be a little seasick."

Chelsea reached out a hand to my forehead and I sat frozen in place. "You do feel a little warm." She pulled the gun from the waistband of her shorts. I'd been wondering where that thing had gone. She motioned with it, pointing towards the door. "Let's go above and get you some fresh air."

I dutifully complied, eager to put some distance between me and the cooler. We emerged from below and I sank into a chair, my mind working to digest the information it had just been given. I felt my stomach heave, and took a deep breath.

"What happened next, Chelsea?"

She sat in the seat opposite me, excitedly describing the demise of her next victim, the unfortunate Jennifer Donnelly. "But by that time, I already had a plan in place," Chelsea said slyly, her tongue running over her teeth. "See that monitor?"

I looked at the small screen mounted to the side of the boat. It looked like a map, with a tiny blip blinking on it. "That's Fred," she said.

I bolted to me feet, moving closer to the blip. "Fred?"

"Yep. Remember a couple of weeks ago, Mazo's was having their annual outdoor party?"

I thought back, nodding.

"You had Fred on a leash, I tripped over him on purpose."

Eyes wide, I kept nodding. I remembered. I had been there to cover the story, so I handed the leash to Siobhan and walked away while she untangled the leash from the person who tripped. Chelsea.

"I pretended to pat Fred and stuck an electronic monitoring device to the under side of his collar with Velcro. I knew you always had him with you when you went jogging, so I'd know exactly where you were," she explained.

This is the where I was supposed to offer compliments, I felt. "Wow, how smart of you! And you did this because?"

Chelsea tilted her head to one side, her laugh raucous in the sea air. "So I could give you the girls, silly. When I killed them, I had them mixed up with you." She twirled a finger in circles next to her head. "But they weren't really you, of course, so I wanted you to see what you had to look forward to. It wasn't enough, killing them, or even you finding them."

The boat bobbed up and down in the ocean, secured by the anchor I'd heard going overboard. I knew I had to stay calm if I wanted to live. Seagulls hovered overhead like sea vultures waiting to feed.

"It got pretty bad at the Calhoun party. I couldn't stand being there watching you take your little notes and chatting with everyone. I thought it was you going up the back staircase and I followed you to the bathroom, but it wasn't you. Stupid girl tried to scream so I, you know." She made a swift movement with her hand.

I swallowed, keeping my eyes on the gun she kept gesturing with. My breathing was shallow, but I kept my face devoid of emotion. "What about the last girl, Chelsea? Why did you bring her to my house?"

She waved dismissively. "Oh, her. She was a fluke, not even a surfer. She was at the marina, varnishing a boat, and something about her reminded me of you." Chelsea eyed me fondly. "I invited her for a beer, but she wasn't you, either, so I choked her, too. But you stopped going for your morning runs, so I just brought her right to you, pulled right out in the creek in my skiff." She gestured to the small vessel attached to her cruiser.

"Why surfers, Chelsea?" I knew I should quit while I was ahead, but my curious streak didn't know when to stop.

The wind shifted, picking up speed and ruffling Chelsea's sort hair. I caught the snap of her eyes as they flared up, but she cooled them, lids drooping so I couldn't read her. She stared at me like that for a while, perspiration forming above her upper lip. I sat transfixed, knowing I was running out of time.

She spoke softly. "Because that's how I think of you, Kell. Out in the water, crowds of people around you, having a wonderful time and never even knowing I was alive. It's how you always were."

She stood up, gun in hand. "Come on, I have something down below I want you to try on," she said, turning towards the cabin door.

I slowly got to my feet, silently said a prayer, then charged her with all my might. Stunned, she slipped and pointed the gun at me. It went off, shattering the windshield behind me then clattered to the deck. All five feet four inches of me propelled her on, slamming her in to the railing, but she was stronger and grabbed my hair and yanked my head back. The gleam of the knife glittered in the sunlight as I felt a searing pain like fire in my thigh as she brought it down.

"You bitch," Chelsea screeched as I fell to the ground, holding my leg. She lunged for her gun and I saw the glint of metal as it came crashing down on my skull.

CHAPTER TWENTY-NINE

At first I thought I was truly dead but then some sort of consciousness crept back, allowing me to experience a ferocious, excruciating throbbing in my skull. In brief snatches my eyes would open to see the blurred, blood-red sun above bathing the turquoise sky in a gold radiance, an incredibly brilliant Southern sky my eyes simply could not bear to see as they closed again and again. I wanted to slip back to wherever it was I came from.

Far, far away came the sounds of singing. Some off tune, high-pitched soloist crooning, giggling and whistling. The voice grew louder until I knew it was close by.

"Wake up, Kell, look what I made! Open your eyes, dammit." This came accompanied by a swift kick to my leg. The pain was intense and I screamed.

"See? Another letter, I just finished it. This one will be attached to you when you're discovered. See?"

I squinted at the sheet of white paper dangling above my head and saw the cut out letters but couldn't read them. Chelsea was shaking the paper in my face and I tried to sit up but couldn't move. This realization produced the proper amount of adrenaline to rush through my body and I struggled to raise my head.

I was on the deck of the boat at the rear, flat on my back on a surfboard, held in place by the familiar boat rope. A flash of purple confirmed my suspicion that I had on the rash guard. I moaned, and my head found an unyielding fiberglass pillow.

"Yessiree, got you all dressed and ready to go," Chelsea said, her face close to mine. "Here's a secret. They only had their bottoms cut off so people would think the killer was a guy. Pretty smart, huh? I left your shorts on for now, manners and all that."

She stood up and twirled around the deck, executing a playful pirouette. My eyes closed again, and I wished for the oblivion that would hide the pain. My left thigh pulsated where the knife had entered and I detected the coppery smell of blood. Chelsea had danced herself up to the bow railing and I heard loud splashes.

"There go your shoes! Here's your shirt, lost at sea," she sang out.

Quickly she was at my side again, talking to me from some far off place. It was a time of half-light for me, a kind of suspended-in-air time. I groaned as she kicked me again, in my ribs this time. I felt spittle drip down my cheek.

"...only this time you'll be dead," came through as she spit on me one more time, whirled and stomped below deck.

I forced my eyes open to catch a glimpse of the wondrous heavens above, wondering what it would be like to become a part of the afterlife, because I had no doubts about my destiny. I was bound to the surfboard, barely conscious, with a lunatic kidnapper. Killer. Reality time, Scarlett.

There was an almost imperceptible swish of seawater behind my head and I tilted my eyes in that direction. Okay, so maybe now I was dead, and this was one of the angels assigned to escort me on. One with dripping, long red hair and a dagger between her teeth.

Siobhan was hoisting herself noiselessly over the back of the boat, clad only in her bra and underwear. She knelt down beside me and took the dagger out of her mouth.

"Didn't have time to shop for a bathing suit," she whispered grimly, her green eyes flashing.

"How....," I tried, my tongue not working in my mouth.

"Shhh, later," Siobhan said. Footsteps pounded up the stairs from below and she moved quietly like a gazelle and crouched behind the captain's chair.

Chelsea flung the door open and stood with her gun pointing at me. She was breathing rapidly, staring at me crazily. Slowly, she walked over and knelt down beside me, placing the gun on the deck.

"Now I'm starting to hear things and I don't like that," she said, her breath warm and acrid in my face. I felt hands at my throat, caressing at first and then squeezing, fingers pressing down until I gasped for air. "It's time, Kell."

It was quite easy to fade away as I was already half way there. I quit struggling and the weight around my throat grew tighter until the back spots became white spots and I hear a blood-curdling scream.

There was a loud thump as Siobhan sailed through the air and tackled Chelsea, emitting war cries that would surely make her Celtic ancestors proud. From my awkward position I witnessed completely unladylike gnashing of teeth and wrestling, until the two women found their swords and began slicing at each other mercilessly. Well, Chelsea had her knife and Siobhan her dagger, but they were dueling like the pirates of old. I was doing my best to stay out of the way, which meant I was stuck to the board and all, when Chelsea suddenly lunged in my direction, grabbed my hair to expose my neck and brought the sharp edge of her knife to my throat. I gasped as the sting of the blade touched down.

Just as quickly Siobhan screamed "NO!" And dove for the gun Chelsea had left on the deck and took aim. The single shot caught Chelsea in the middle of the forehead, a point I can attest to as she fell beside me with the gaping hole near my face.

Siobhan hurried below and emerged with a cloth of some sort, which she held at my neck while cutting through the boat rope anchoring me to the surfboard. She moved my arms until they more or less propped the towel against my neck, then hoisted the anchor and started the engines. She didn't bother to move Chelsea so I had a spectacular view as we raced through the waters. Until I blacked out for good, that is.

CHAPTER THIRTY

It was the following day, or possibly the day after that, and I was now propped up in my hospital bed with nicely starched white sheets pulled tightly around me and an IV in my forearm hooked to a tube dripping some concoction into my body. I'd lost a lot of blood, between the stab in my thigh and the beginnings of my very own ear-to-ear slice under my chin. Both had been neatly sutured and bandaged and were not causing me much discomfort thanks to the very thoughtful nurse who kept me plied with pain medication. They had to be careful, I understood, because of the severe concussion I had to boot. There were a staggering amount of flowers covering every available surface and the floor, sent by folks from Folly who had heard of my misfortune. And here I thought they only read my articles to make sure I spelled their names right. Seems they actually care.

I was finally alone, as visiting hours were officially over. I joked about installing a revolving door earlier as people came and went. Mid and Siobhan, of course, Chief Stoney and the entire Folly Beach police force, George and Bonnie McLeod, Beau and Laura, Ludmilla and Murphy. Everyone from *The Archipelago*, even Linski and Holly. When I first came to I spent a few moments as Dorothy from the Wizard of Oz with familiar faces surrounding me, wanting to exclaim it was a dream, just a dream, but those moments quickly faded when I was brought up to speed about my adventure.

Siobhan described returning to Murphy's boat and discovering my black bag, but not me, and seeing the boat with Chelsea at the wheel pulling away from the dock. She conferred with the blind fellow, Jake, who told her it was indeed Miss Chester's boat now that her Daddy had died, and yes, he did hear two sets of footsteps passing him on the creaky pier. Lucky for me Siobhan heeded her keen gut feelings and dashed back to Murphy's boat where I had left the keys in the ignition. She followed us at a distance, stopping when Chelsea threw anchor and watched through binoculars as I tried to escape and all. After calling the police station, she swam from Murphy's boat to Chelsea's in nothing but her undergarments, which caused quite a commotion when she ran the boat aground in front of the Holiday Inn to meet the ambulance and police cars that had already arrived.

I remember nothing of this story Siobhan relayed to me and which she would relay in its entirety for months to come for anyone who would listen, I was sure of it. Her deadly accurate shot had saved my life, and she was destined to become a hero in the eyes of our town. I'd already heard her entertaining the police force with vivid descriptions of her duel with the killer. She's claiming to be a descendant of Anne Bonny, the famous woman pirate born in Cork, Ireland in 1700, which is quite possible and makes for a very colorful picture when you hear Siobhan tell it.

Although I haven't seen him yet I have a roommate down the hall. When the police searched Chelsea's large house, which sits at the west end of Folly, they discovered Cyrus Davis handcuffed and chained to a steel bar welded to a steel door in a small, hidden room. He'd been there since Friday, when Chelsea had apparently lured him over for a beer and then shocked him with a stun gun and trapped him. Seems she thought Cyrus was my current love interest and was deciding how to do away with him when she was interrupted. Cyrus had told Chief Stoney some pretty horrendous tales of the days he spent listening to Chelsea ramble. According to Chelsea, she hadn't been an only child after all. She'd simply drowned her younger sister in the bathtub when they were little.

The chief had discovered more than Cyrus at the house. He found numerous newspaper articles dating back to three years ago from a town in Georgia covering an unnamed killer who was strangling women with straight black hair. He also found pictures of these unfortunate women, dead, along with hundreds of pictures of a slightly Asian looking woman with shiny black hair. He was in touch with the authorities in Georgia to help tie up the unsolved case.

So I wasn't Chelsea's first irritation in life, which helped a little when I thought of the four dead women who looked like me. I was her last, however, and as gruesome as her demise had been, perhaps justice had been served. I knew in time I would stop thinking of her beside me on the deck, finally stopped from killing again, but for now I shivered alone in my hospital room.

I was starting to doze off when my door creaked open and a long shadow fell across the room. My eyes were wide and I saw a rather large head poke around the door questioningly.

"Go ahead, go in," someone whispered. "Come on, we're trying to be sneaky here."

The head entered my room followed by the rest of him, and Fred jumped up on to the single bed and looked around for a place he could sit. Not finding one he sat anyways directly on my legs. I winced and moved my left leg to the side, and he sort of flopped down and inspected me. I must have passed, because he immediately began snoring.

"How'd you get him in here," I asked, my voice cracking. The pain in my neck made it difficult to talk.

Mid turned a chair around so he was straddling it and rested his chin on the back. Over his shoulder, I saw two pretty young nurses giggling as they closed my door, waving as they left. Oh.

"Your parents and Aidan are on their way, well, your parents are and Aidan should be here in a week or so," Mid told me. "Your mom and dad are in Scotland visiting your grandparents, so it'll be a day at least."

Tears stung my eyes and I wiped them away with the back of my hand. I couldn't remember the last time my family was all in one place. Next time I didn't intend to be the reason we reunited, at least not in this manner, but at least I'd see them all.

"Oh, yeah, this is from Bonnie McLeod," Mid said, handing me a note.

I read it and grinned, as laughing hurt too much. Dear, sweet Bonnie had no time for tragedies befalling mere mortals.

"What's it say?" Mid asked, grinning, too.

I handed him the sheet of paper.

"So, she just wants to remind you the boa constrictor is still loose on the island," he said, shaking his head.

"Yep," I replied. "Which only means one thing."

Mid raised his eyebrows. "What?"

I sat up straighter and yanked at the crisp hospital sheets. Fred grunted in his sleep and held his position.

"It means I have to hurry up and get out of here. There's a whole lot of reporting that needs done on Folly," I answered.

Made in the USA